TANDEM

For a Few Dollars More

There were two of them. The tall stranger they called the Man With No Name, and the grey-haired Colonel with the fancy guns. Each moving across the violent West, killing outlaws for a price. Each unaware of the other.

Until El Indio. The Mexican bandit, worth $10,000 dead or alive. Then the two hunters stalked the same prey.

Their plan was simple. The younger man would join up with El Indio's gang—then lure the bandit to the Colonel's waiting ambush.

It was going to be easy. If the sadistic El Indio didn't kill the tall stranger first . . . If the Colonel's ambush didn't include his hard-eyed young partner . . . If the Man With No Name didn't double deal them all . . .

For a Few Dollars More

Joe Millard

TANDEM
14 Gloucester Road, London SW7

First published in the United States by
Universal Publishing and Distributing Corporation, 1967

Published in Great Britain by
Universal-Tandem Publishing Co. Ltd., 1968
Reprinted April 1969
Reprinted 1970
Reprinted 1971
Reprinted May 1972

Released through United Artists

Cover photograph by permission of United Artists

Made and printed in Great Britain by
The Garden City Press Ltd., Letchworth, Herts. SG6 1JS

CHAPTER 1

NORMALLY, the sheriff of Tucumcari was not a man easily spooked. But when he glanced up from his morning mail and discovered the stranger standing beyond his desk it gave him a start.

Not that strangers were a novelty, but the sheriff was accustomed to having their arrival announced by the clumping of boot heels and the creak of loosely laid floor boards. This man's coming had been as soundless as if he had materialised out of thin air.

He stood with his back turned, examining a reward poster on the wall. It bore the sketch of a heavy, brutish face and the customary legend:

WANTED

DEAD OR ALIVE

"Red" Cavanagh

$2,000 Reward

The sheriff curbed his annoyance and studied the stranger's back. The man was tall—a good six-feet-four or better—and lean as a bull whip. He wore a brown-and-white poncho in the Mexican fashion, with the head poked through a slit in the centre and the fringed ends falling almost to the knees, front and back. His hat was broad-brimmed and flat-crowned in the Texas style.

With a faint sense of relief, the sheriff noted that neither the tip of a holster nor a tie-down thong was visible below the poncho's fringe. At least the stranger was not wearing his gun low-slung and tied down in the manner of a gunfighter on the prod and itching to kill.

The sheriff cleared his throat. "I didn't hear you come in, friend."

The stranger continued to study the poster with no indication that he had heard. The sheriff scowled with rising irritation.

"Is there something I can do for you, mister?"

The man turned then, quick on his feet as a cat. He was about thirty—perhaps less—with deep-set eyes narrowed to slits and a stubborn jaw covered by a sparse beard. His face seemed pleasant enough but was as expressionless as an Indian's, as if he had long ago learned to mask any thought or feeling. Only a faint glint in the slitted eyes gave the sheriff an uneasy impression of controlled but hair-trigger violence.

Without speaking, holding the sheriff's eyes with an unwinking stare, the stranger lifted the front of the poncho and tossed it over his shoulder. His gun was there, all right, a heavy .44, and although he wore it high on his hip, the grips had the well-worn sheen of frequent use.

Silent and deliberate, the man reached inside a short sheepskin vest and took a stubby Mexican *cigarro* from a shirt pocket. He helped himself to a wooden match from the sheriff's desk. When the cigar was lit to his satisfaction, he spoke for the first time.

"Cavanagh," he said. "The deal still open?"

The sheriff started again. "You're a bounty killer."

"Bounty *hunter*," the stranger corrected. "The notice says dead *or* alive."

"They all do," the sheriff snapped, "but I never seen one brung in that way."

"I let the other fellow call the deal. He can have it either way."

A faint chill brushed the hairs on the sheriff's neck. "As far as I know, the reward's still open. Unless, of course, somebody gunned him down today, which I doubt. Red don't kill easy."

"Cash?" No inflection, no wasted words.

"On delivery."

"It's a big country."

"Well-l-l," the sheriff rasped a thumbnail along his stubbled jaw. "If I was to go after Cavanagh—which I sure as hell ain't—I'd start looking over at White Rocks. He's got plenty of friends there."

"Thanks."

"Wait!" The sheriff scrambled through a littered desk drawer and found a chewed stub of pencil. "If you're aiming to try for the two thousand, I'll have to have your name."

"Why?"

"For my records, dammit. I have to keep records. If you earn the reward, I got to report who I paid it to. And if you don't . . ." The corners of his mouth quirked downward, "I'll know what name to put on the cemetery headboard."

No reply, no change of expression. The sheriff

glared angrily, then bent down to search a bottom drawer for the paper he was seeking. "Everybody's got some kind of a name, dammit. I got no time to go chasing around to make sure the name a man gives me is the one he was borned to. So just tell me one I can put down on my . . ."

He straightened up, his voice trailing off as he discovered he had been addressing an empty office. The stranger had gone, as abruptly and soundlessly as he had appeared.

The sheriff swore savagely. Then, moistening the stub of pencil, he scrawled *Red Cavanagh—$2,000* at the top of a form and, beneath it, *Man With No Name.*

CHAPTER 2

EXCEPT for the weathered outcropping that had inspired its name, White Rocks might have been any of a thousand drab western towns. A collection of unpainted shanties and false-fronted business establishments clustered around the intersection of two wagon trails. From the largest came the steady thumping of an off-key piano, the clink of glassware and the din of drunken voices. A dozen or more saddled horses drooped patiently along the hitchrail in front.

The hunter without a name reined in at the edge of town and sat for a long time, studying the street and the buildings, his face devoid of expression. Overhead, black, scurrying clouds were laced with barbed lightning. Thunder rumbled and a spatter of rain stung the hunter's cheek.

His horse, a handsome, long-legged bay with white stockings, shifted uneasily. The man swung down, looped the reins over his arm and got out one of the short *cigarros*. He got it going nicely, only to have it hiss out a moment later as the storm broke in all its fury with blinding sheets of wind-driven rain.

Head down to the storm, the hunter groped his way to the saloon hitchrail and tied the bay with its rump to the wind. Under the shelter of the saloon's wooden canopy he paused to shake the rain from the tight-woven poncho and to thoroughly dry and warm his gun hand. To a gunfighter, a rain-slick palm could be as fatal as an empty holster.

He stood for a long minute, looking over the top of the swinging doors, studying every detail of the big, rambling saloon and the mob that jammed it to the rafters. There were a number of hard-cases in the crowd but none touched a responsive chord in his cash-register memory of "wanted" men, nor did any resemble the sketch of Red Cavanagh. He ignored the swarm of bar girls in brief-skirted, low-cut outfits who squirmed through the jam, delivering drinks to tables, dodging the amorous grabs of some of the drunks, honeying up to the more affluent patrons.

Beyond the long bar, a short flight of steps led to a small, elevated alcove where a group of men hunched around a poker table. A grizzled man wearing a sheriff's star on his shirt pocket walked slowly around the table, puffing a fat cigar and looking over the players' hands.

He said something that brought brief laughter, then came down the steps just as the hunter stepped through the swinging doors. Their glances met and locked, the lawman's eyes bright with wary curiosity.

As they came abreast the hunter put out a hand. "How about a light?"

The sheriff looked startled, then held out his lighted cigar. The tall man bent to it, sucking fire into his rain-sodden *cigarro*. When it glowed to his satisfaction, he straightened.

"Red Cavanagh. Where would a man find him?"

The sheriff's eyes were suddenly hooded and unrevealing. After a long moment his head tilted almost imperceptibly towards the alcove. "Up at that table. The one with his back to you."

He watched until the tall stranger started up the steps, then spun around and hurried out through the swinging doors, almost at a run. Across the room, the piano player missed a note.

Red Cavanagh was a squat, thick-bodied bull of a man with cold blue eyes and bristling sandy hair above a narrow forehead. He had just finished cutting the cards and slid the pack to his left. As the dealer reached for it, the hunter stepped soundlessly to the table between them, covering the cards with his own left hand.

The dealer started up, his eyes hot with quick anger. "What the hell you think you're . . ." Then he caught the full impact of the intruder's cold stare and the words sputtered out. He sagged back into the chair, his face going slack.

Cavanagh twisted around to gape up at the impassive face of the stranger, his dull wits struggling to cope with the shock of complete surprise. He shot a bewildered look at the other players, then returned his gaze to the silent interloper. His tongue slid out to moisten dry lips. The blue eyes were more puzzled than alarmed.

Down in the main saloon, the drunken tumult abruptly died. The only sound was the steady rasping snore of a man asleep with his face on a beer-puddled table. In the alcove, the other players slid out of their chairs and faded carefully back from the table.

Holding Red's eyes with an unwinking gaze, the stranger picked up the pack and began to deal one-handed—a card to the hunted, a card to the hunter. He dealt slowly, deliberately, building up the nerve-clawing tension until the soft slap of a card was like a thunderclap in the stillness.

When each had a five-card hand, the hunter put down the pack and shot a quick glance at his cards. He saw two aces, an eight, a five and a seven. Red sucked in a ragged breath, wet his lips again and picked up his own hand, cupping the cards from the other's view. A muscle jumped beside his mouth.

Using his left hand, the tall man deftly separated the two aces and discarded the three low cards. He scooped up the pack and waited.

"Two cards," Red said hoarsely, making his own discards. The hand that snatched up the replacements was not quite steady.

With a little yelp of glee, Red triumphantly spread his hand on the table—three kings, a ten and a queen. He leered up at his opponent, gloating.

The other leaned down to spread his own hand. It held three aces, a queen and a jack.

For long, dragging moments Red stared at the winning hand, his big body hunched forward as motionless as a statue. Only a muscle twitched in his cheek. Then he twisted around slowly to look up at the victor.

"I didn't hear you say what the bet was, mister."

The hunter took the chewed remnant of the *cigarro*

from his lips, inspected it carefully and dropped it on the floor. He ground it under his boot and spat out a shred of tobacco. His lips moved in the faintest of humourless smiles.

"Your life, Red."

The outlaw stared at him blankly, scowling as his slow mind groped for the meaning of the words. Then comprehension hit him and he came up, roaring curses, kicking the chair away as he sledged at his enemy with massive fists. The other blocked the blows with elbows and forearms like steel bars and caught Red in a rib-crushing bear hug. Red's immense right hand closed on his adversary's throat like a wolf trap.

Panting, straining, they turned in a grotesque, slow-motion death waltz until their feet tangled with the fallen chair and they went down with a crash that shook the building. The hunter was on top. The hard edge of his open palm sliced in a short, vicious arc that broke the death grip on his throat. They scrambled to their feet, hammering one another.

Red Cavanagh had bull-strength but no skill. The other parried most of the punches, while his own fists methodically made a pulp of the red-head's big face. A solid right sent the outlaw crashing down the steps to the saloon floor. Half-stunned, Red tried to rise, then belatedly remembered his holstered gun.

He had it half-drawn when the flying figure of the hunter slammed down on him, smashing the breath from his lungs, sending the pistol skittering across the floor. Bouncing up, the Man With No Name caught the front of Red's shirt and hauled him erect, rocking his head back and forth with vicious, open-hand slaps. Whirling the heavy figure around, he slammed it against the bar.

"Alive or dead, Red? The choice is yours."

Behind them, the swinging doors flapped softly and a cold, deadly voice said, "Let—Red—go!"

The hunter moved slowly, turning only his head until he could see the owner of the voice. Three hard-bitten toughs stood just inside the doors, covering him with cocked pistols. All three bore the stamp of gun-fighters—the cold eyes, the bared teeth, the tied-down holsters, the boots planted wide for balance.

"Let him go," the tallest said again. "Red, drop down and scramble clear. We'll take care of him for you."

There was not even a flicker of alarm in the face of the hunter, no visible tensing of muscles. One moment he was holding the battered Cavanagh erect, looking impassively over his shoulder at certain death. The next instant he was spinning around, the .44 in his hand, the heel of his left hand slapping the hammer, fanning the gun so fast that the three shots sounded almost as one.

The gun-toughs were literally blasted backward through the swinging doors to sprawl in the mud of the street. Only one got off a shot, and that was the reflex of a man already dead, the bullet smashing harmlessly into the ceiling.

The hunter remained in his half-crouch, his gun still levelled, while he searched the faces of the spectators jammed along the farthest wall. He saw awe, incredulity, naked fear, a furtive darting of eyes toward something behind his back.

When the Man With No Name had let go of Red Cavanagh to make his play, the outlaw had slumped to the floor, then scrambled wildly to get out of the line of fire. Red was behind him now—and so was the gun the outlaw had been forced to drop. The hunter's mind pictured exactly where the weapon had come to rest after skidding away.

Afterwards, a score of witnesses in the saloon were willing to swear that the tall, lean stranger fired behind him, under his left arm, before he had spun far enough around to see his target. That would be impossible, of course, but by the time the stranger had fully turned, Red Cavanagh lay dead on the floor, with one hand on his gun and a bullet hole in his forehead.

The bounty killer raked the crowd again with his chilling stare, then holstered his gun. He hooked a hand into the dead man's belt and straightened. Dragging the heavy body as a man might drag a sack of oats, he strode out, to cash in his two-thousand dollar prize.

The sheriff of White Rocks looked up and froze, his face ashen. The bounty killer watched him in cold silence until drops of sweat began to dot the lawman's forehead.

"Tell me," the stranger said at last, "isn't a sheriff supposed to be courageous, loyal and, above all . . . honest?"

The sheriff wet his lips. "Y-yes. That he is."

Slowly, deliberately, the bounty killer leaned over

and unpinned the nickelled star. He gave the sweating man a last, cold look of scorn and turned to the door.

Outside, the street was alive with knots of men, talking excitedly about the shooting and the fantastic speed and accuracy of the tall stranger. They fell silent as their subject appeared and an old man snatched off his battered hat, as if in a gesture of awe. The bounty killer tossed the badge into the hat.

"You people need a new sheriff," he said, and went on to untie his horse.

He rode out as he had come, nameless, a Man From Nowhere, but he left behind him a legend that would never die.

But some thirty-odd miles to the north and west, a chain of bloody events was being set in motion by a man he had never seen or heard of—a man destined to affect and alter the course of his whole future.

CHAPTER 3

The train crawled steadily southward across the bleak and sun-baked landscape. Midway in the first coach a little man with a thin fox face and a scraggly beard fidgeted on the hard cushion and morosely contemplated his choice of seat-mates. He was a lonely and gregarious little man whose hunger for conversation had been frustrated from the start of his journey.

He had no sooner taken his seat when he was crowded into the corner by a fat and stolid Indian squaw who ignored his hopeful " 'Morning, ma'am. A scorcher of a day, ain't it?"

The facing seat was occupied by a tall, lean, well-dressed stranger and his carpet bag. Unhappily, the stranger had spent his entire time reading a large Bible, holding it up so that not once had the little man even glimpsed the face behind it. Somehow, he had not yet mustered the courage to try breaching that obvious barricade against companionship.

As the conductor came down the aisle, calling, "Tickets! Tickets, ever'body!" the little man dug his from a vest pocket and handed it up. A hard brown hand came from behind the Bible to proffer the pasteboard, then a voice spoke from behind the screen. "Is it far to Tucumcari, Conductor?"

The conductor consulted an enormous gold watch.

"We should pass there in three, four minutes now."

"Thanks."

The little man fairly wriggled with delight and bent forward. "Er—excuse me, Reverend, but I'm afraid you've made a mistake, and a bad one. I couldn't help hearing you're goin' to Tucumcari. Now, I peddle goods around here so I know these trains well, and I have to tell you you're on the wrong one. I think the nearest stop to Tucumcari would be Amarillo. You'd have to get off at Santa Fe and return by way of Amarillo to get right where you want to go . . ."

His voice trailed off as the Bible was slowly lowered to reveal a hard, sun-browned wedge of face. High, protruding cheekbones framed eyes of so light a brown that they could almost be called sorrel. The "reverend" was holding a curved bulldog pipe of yellow meerschaum in his teeth and a thin trickle of blue smoke spiralled upward.

Silently and without expression, the stranger studied the little man as if he were some kind of insect that dared come near. Under that chilling stare, the little man squirmed and blurted desperately. "Th-this train —uh—doesn't stop at Tucumcari."

The stranger closed the Bible and put it into the carpet bag. He glanced out the window, then stood up. As he did so, his long frock coat fell open to reveal the biggest hand-gun the little man had ever seen. Its barrel was a good fourteen inches in length, which would give it almost the range and accuracy of a rifle. It was holstered high in front of the man's left hip, the butt angled sharply to the right for a lightning-fast, cross-belly draw. The little man gaped at it with bulging eyes.

The stranger took the pipe from his mouth and spoke for the first time. "This train will stop at Tucumcari."

He reached up and jerked the emergency cord dangling from the coach ceiling. From up forward in the engine cab came the brassy jangle of a bell, followed by the screech of tortured metal as brake shoes bit down on iron wheels. Over this came the thunderous roar of venting steam.

The car bucked and lurched. The little man was hurled on to the lap of the squaw with a force that sent them both to the floor. By the time they got untangled, the stranger had vanished.

Outside, the engineer and fireman leaped from the locomotive cab as the conductor swung down from the rear coach. He ran forward, bellowing, "What happened? What the hell's the big idea of stopping like that?"

"Somebody pulled the emergency cord," the engineer bawled back.

"I'd like to get my hands on the son of a . . ." the conductor's voice sputtered out as the baggage car door slid open. A cleated loading ramp was shoved out and the man in the frock coat appeared, leading a magnificent coal-black saddle horse.

The conductor charged forward, his beefy face purple with rage. "Look here, mister, you can't just pull the emergency cord and get off any damn where you please. What makes you think you got the right to stop my train? If you wanted to get off at Tucumcari, you shoulda . . ."

The tall man stopped and turned. For the first time, the conductor saw the enormous gun; his belligerence evaporated. He gulped and finished lamely, "What I mean to say, sir, is that the railroad company'd be mighty pleased to make any arrangement in advance when a passenger wants to get off here. They'd see to it that the train stopped."

"The train *did* stop," the tall man said mildly, "and I *did* get off. I'm much obliged." He tipped his black hat politely and went on, leading the black horse, leaving the conductor with his mouth agape.

The conductor was more fortunate than he knew. Not many men had bawled angrily at Colonel Douglas Mortimer of Carolina and survived to remember it. Once known as the deadliest shot in the Army, Colonel Mortimer had, since leaving the service, found a great many opportunities to keep his lethal skill from growing rusty.

Now he was heading towards a reward poster nailed to the wall of the rickety Tucumcari depot. It was offering a reward of $1,000, dead or alive, for a murderer by the name of Guy Callaway. Some joker with a pencil had added two crudely scrawled zeros to the printed reward figure.

As the Colonel studied the poster, a fat man wearing a green eye-shade leaned out from the depot ticket window, grinning. "Guy hisself added on them two extry zeros t'other day. He was spittin' mad when he came back to town and seen how little they was offerin' for him. He sure weren't flattered none. He says to me, standin' right where you are now, he says, 'A measly thousand bucks for me is an insult. I'm worth one helluva lot more'n that.' So he ups and makes it a hundred thousand, then and there." The ticket seller chuckled. "Not that it matters how much it says. There's nobody got the guts to go agin' Guy Callaway's gun for any amount o' money."

The Colonel looked coldly at the ticket agent for a long moment, then turned and carefully peeled the poster from the wall. Rolling it, he tucked it inside the frock coat. The fat railroadman seemed to wilt. He gulped and added hoarsely, "Leastwise, there wasn't nobody til' now."

Tucumcari's lone saloon was virtually empty of patrons when Colonel Mortimer pushed through the swinging doors. The heavy-set bartender pushed his face into a hearty smile and bustled up, carrying a bottle of whisky and a glass. The Colonel's hand sent them spinning down the bar. He got out the reward poster and spread it, facing the bartender.

"Where is he?"

The bartender's eyes were suddenly veiled. He shrugged and grunted unintelligibly. The Colonel's lips thinned.

"I asked you a question."

The bartender turned away, went down the bar and returned carrying a stack of glasses, deliberately ignoring the man in the frock coat. As he came by, the Colonel's left hand shot out, caught him by the shirt front and dragged him halfway across the mahogany. The bartender found himself staring into a pair of blazing tawny eyes that reminded him of the eyes of a mountain lion about to spring on its prey.

"Where—is—he?"

The Colonel let go and the bartender straightened, his face chalk-white and sheened with cold sweat. He swallowed heavily, threw a frightened glance around the saloon, then rolled his eyes straight upward, towards the ceiling.

"I wouldn't have no idea where he'd be right now, mister."

The Colonel smiled thinly, swung away from the bar and went up a stairway, carrying the rolled poster in his left hand. At the top he stood for a moment; he was at the end of a hallway lined with bedrooms. All the doors were closed but from beyond one came the sound of voices and the splashing of water. The Colonel tiptoed to the door.

A man's voice growled, "Hold still, damn yuh!"

"But, Guy . . .," the woman's voice protested.

"Hold still, I said."

"But you hurt me with those hands of yours."

"Then do what I tell yuh!"

The woman giggled, then cried, "Oh! Now, see? You've made me drop the soap."

The man laughed. "Wait. I'll get it for yuh."

There was more splashing and the woman shrieked, "Eeee! You're tickling me . . . *Guy! Look!* Wh-what's that?"

That was the unrolled reward poster the Colonel

was quietly shoving under the door. He straightened and stepped aside, flattening his lean body against the wall outside the room.

Inside there was dead silence. Then the man's voice burst into wild cursing. A volley of pistol shots boomed and slugs tore through the door at the height to shatter the chest of a man unwary enough to be standing in front of it. The gunfire stopped and there was a rasp of a window sash being shoved up.

The immense, long-barrelled gun was in the Colonel's hand and cocked before his boot hit the riddled door and sent it crashing open. Across the room, a young woman sat in a tin bathtub. She screamed and made a token attempt to cover her nakedness as the Colonel ran past her to the open window. He leaned out just in time to see a stocky man, carrying a jacket and saddlebags, drop from the end of the balcony and vanish around a corner of the building.

The Colonel whirled and strode to the door, then paused to doff his flat-crowned black hat. He bowed. "My apologies, ma'am."

He burst out of the saloon in time to see his quarry leaping on to a running horse, already too far away for even his long-barrelled weapon. The Colonel whirled to where his own horse stood at the rail. On the side of the saddle was what appeared to be a long bedroll, covered with canvas and held in the middle by a buckskin thong.

He jerked the thong and the object unrolled with a snap. Inside the canvas, held by spring clips, were two finely inlaid rifles—a shotgun and a heavy buffalo gun. The Colonel snatched one of the rifles, cocked it and fired in one smooth motion. At the far end of the street the racing horse went down in a cloud of dust, sending its rider rolling.

The fugitive lay motionless for a moment, stunned. Then he got to his feet and stumbled, gun in hand, to look down at his horse. The Colonel raised his rifle again, just as his quarry looked up.

Callaway saw the rifle and skittered crazily backward, ducking and weaving. But when the rifle cracked again, he went down heavily, sprawling in the dust. The Colonel turned and calmly put the rifle back. He rolled up the canvas carefully and retied the securing thong.

When he turned again, Callaway was on his feet. One side of his shirt was dark with blood but he still had the strength to stagger towards his pursuer, his face contorted with rage.

"Goddam yuh!" he yelled. "I'll kill yuh for this! Goddam yuh! Goddam yuh!"

His gun blazed and bucked in his hand. The slug kicked up a spurt of dust, directly in line with the frock-coated figure but a dozen feet short. The Colonel regarded the spot dispassionately, then drew the long-barrelled pistol. From inside his coat he brought out a rifle stock of curious construction and calmly fitted the butt of his long pistol into its curved end.

The stumbling outlaw fired again, the fountain of dust erupting no more than six feet in front of the Colonel's boots. Mortimer neither moved nor glanced up, but went on calmly and methodically tightening the set of thumbscrews that held the pistol butt rigidly to the stock.

He finished and slowly settled the butt against his shoulder as a third bullet hit just in front of one boot. His dark, craggy face showed no trace of emotion as he cocked the pistol and took deliberate time settling the sights squarely on the approaching killer.

Unmoving, the Colonel let the gunman get off another shot, the slug going between his planted boots. Only then did he squeeze off a single shot. Callaway went down, a bullet hole in the precise centre of his forehead.

The Colonel disassembled his curious weapon and stowed the parts away before walking to his victim. Hoisting the dead man by the belt, he dragged him down the street toward a sign reading "Sheriff's Office." He opened the creaking door.

"Where do I cash this one in?"

The sheriff of Tucumcari heaved his bulk up from behind his desk. "I'd begun to think nobody was ever going to claim that thousand." He lumbered to a small iron safe in the corner.

The Colonel put away the cash and tipped his head toward the reward notice on the wall. "Anybody collected the two thousand on that Red Cavanagh yet?"

"Not that I've heard, but there was another feller in the same line o' business as you askin' about him a day or so ago. He rode on toward White Rocks when I told him that was where Red generally hung out."

Colonel Mortimer's eyes narrowed. "What was the fellow's name?"

The sheriff made a wry face. "He didn't seem to want to say. The look he give me when I asked him for it kinda took away any notion I had of pushin' him on the matter."

The Colonel tipped his hat politely. "Thank you, sheriff. I hope we meet again soon."

He rode south out of Tucumcari in the direction of White Rocks but his mind was not on Red Cavanagh or the two thousand dollars in bounty he represented. While the thick bulk of the reward money in his pocket was pleasant to feel, it represented only a means to him and not an end.

Over the years he had earned and spent many such bounties, but each had served only to carry him a few steps further along a dark and fearful trail. One day that trail would come to its blazing end at the feet of the one person whose killing would fulfil the long ordeal.

The image of that person filled his tormented memory, as it always did between the brief moments of violence that supported his search. He could not bring himself to call that image a man. An insane monster, a savage animal whose sport was torture and killing without reason or mercy. A mad thing to be hunted down and ruthlessly destroyed.

Some day that would be the destiny of Colonel Douglas Mortimer and no man would rob him of that fulfilment. Not even a rival bounty killer.

CHAPTER 4

In the first pale grey of dawn the prison had the grotesque appearance of a handful of children's blocks, flung carelessly together on the desert floor. The original structure had been simply a large, bare cube of sun-baked adobe, its walls dotted with massively barred doors and windows, looking out on to narrow balconies that were little more than catwalks.

As the prison population grew, more cubes were added. Most of these were of differing sizes and heights, so that a man attempting to traverse the flat roofs would need the agility of a mountain goat. There was always a heavily armed guard on each separate roof level. More guards paced the outer stairways and inner halls.

The prison was known, with justification, as the toughest and most impregnable in the South-west. Its iron bars had been especially forged to turn the sharpest cutting tool. Its adobe walls, two feet and more in thickness, could absorb the impact of a cannon ball or the fury of a dynamite blast without yielding. Through the years, its security had never been breached nor even seriously threatened, and perhaps the guards had grown careless.

Carelessness here could prove a fatal error, for the prison housed the most savage desperadoes spawned by a savage land. But the worst of these was no more than a naughty child by comparison with the bandit chief known as Indio, lodged in the strongest cell on the top floor.

For eighteen dragging months Indio had raged around the confines of that cell like a caged animal while the territorial authorities debated his fate. It was rumoured, with considerable truth, that the law was afraid to mete out the hanging he so richly deserved. To do so would surely invite bloody vengeance from his gang, which had been held together and directed by his second-in-command and only confidant. A man would have to be a complete fool not to shiver at the very prospect of facing so vicious and inhuman a pack of torturers and killers-for-sport.

In the thin dawn light, Indio lay on his bunk, flat on his back, powerful hands laced across his middle. His swarthy face was covered by his broad *sombrero* and his chest rose and fell with the regularity of a man deep in sleep. But beneath the *sombrero* his eyes were open. As they followed the furtive movements of his cell mate, across the room, they glittered like the eyes of a snake.

Indio's fellow-prisoner was an old man, his leathery face almost buried in an unkempt tangle of hair and beard. He had slipped from his bunk at the first light to sit for a long time, peering suspiciously about.

When he was finally satisfied that Indio was really asleep, the old man fumbled under the dirty blankets of his bunk and brought out a small object that glowed a pale white in the deep shadows. It was a rectangle of moulded adobe, about the size of a brick but with strange lines scrawled on its surface and curious protrusions here and there.

Stealing furtive, wary glances at Indio's motionless figure, the old man got a pinch of white dust from a buckskin pouch, moistened it with saliva and kneaded it into a soft ball. He stuck the ball into the adobe object and began to shape it with deft fingers.

Suddenly, from somewhere outside the barred window came the faintest whisper of alien sound. The old man froze. With swift movement he thrust the white object out of sight under the blanket. He got up and tiptoed to the barred door, leaning close to see as far as he could along the narrow outside balcony.

Indio, too, heard the wisp of sound. Under the *sombrero* his eyes went wide and a thin smile touched his lips. The old man came back to his bunk and sat down, his eyes darting nervously from Indio to the door.

On the flat roof of the lowest prison wing, a guard paced sleepily, his rifle slung over his shoulder. The eastern sky was bursting into colour but on the roof the shadows were still deep. The guard could not see the brown hand that gripped the edge of the low wall, almost under his feet. He stood yawning, staring out toward the breaking day.

Clinging with one hand, the intruder flattened against the outer wall and used his other hand to take a pebble from his pocket and flip it up on to the roof. It landed with a faint clatter and the guard spun around, grabbing for his rifle.

The intruder came over the wall in a silent rush. His left hand shot around to cover the guard's nose and mouth while his right drove a long knife into the man's back. The guard thrashed wildly for a moment, then went limp. The intruder let the body down softly, then whirled around to help two companions clamber on to the roof. Crouching low, the three ran to a wall edging the next, higher roof level.

They were men of a stripe, fiercely whiskered, savage, ruthless. All wore their guns low and tied down, with knives and extra pistols tucked into their belts, and spare bullets glistening from crossed bandoliers. These were men who lived and died by their guns, men to whom only gold was sacred.

One straightened to peer cautiously over a wall. A guard, with his back turned, was pacing towards the opposite side of the roof. The man scrambled over and darted behind a chimney as the guard turned and started back.

From the wall where the other two intruders waited, came a sharp scraping noise, loud in the dawn hush. The guard ran towards the sound, unslinging his rifle. He looked down, his eyes bulging at the sight of the waiting pair. His mouth was still opening to bawl the alarm when the blade drove through his back and into his heart.

The killer fumbled inside the guard's jacket and brought out an enormous iron key. Straightening, he waved his *sombrero* and other men came swarming up on the roof. In a silent pack, they all ran to the corner and peered down. Directly beneath, a narrow open balcony ran the full length of the building, with no guards in sight. Like rats swarming off a sinking ship, the men swung over and dropped noiselessly down.

In Indio's cell, the old man jumped as the key grated and the barred door swung open. He started to get up, then shrank back as one of the bandits gestured fiercely. The old man huddled there, staring with bulging eyes as the gang crowded in.

The last man to enter was big, thick-bodied, with a great belly bulging out between gunbelt and bandoliers. An ugly knife-scar ran down from beside his left eye to be lost in the greasy thicket of his beard. His black hair hung in lank strings and the twisted ends of his moustache dangled to his chin. His beaded vest was thick with dust and sweat and the dark stains of dried blood.

Indio sat up. "Nino," he said to his lieutenant. "How are you, *amigo*?"

"Better," the heavy man growled, "now I see you again."

"It took you long enough to get here," Indio said.

"Without your brain," Nino said, "all plans take longer."

Indio uttered a sharp, barking laugh and snapped his fingers. "Hughie!"

The bandit who had knifed the guards took a second pistol from his belt and tossed it across. Indio caught it skilfully, spun the cylinder and stood up. His swarthy face creased in a humourless grin and his dark, liquid eyes glowed.

He stepped across to where the old man stood trembling against the wall. His smile broadened.

"Adios, amigo. Hasta luego!" he said, and shot his cellmate through the heart. So close was the range that the muzzle blast set the tattered shirt afire.

Bending down, Indio ripped the smouldering cloth apart and picked up a folded paper. He fumbled under the dirty blanket, pulled out the small white adobe object and tossed it to Nino. "Guard that with your life, *amigo.*" He jerked his head sharply. *"Move!"*

The crashing echoes of the gunshot had destroyed all hope of slipping away unseen. Indio's men ran down the length of the balcony, boots clattering loudly, to a narrow spiral staircase. From below came the scuffling of boots and the sharp bark of commands.

Three guards came charging into view, their guns at ready. They literally ran into a wall of lead from bandit guns and went down in a limp heap. The pack hurdled the bodies and ran down into a broad corridor. A half-dozen guards were struggling to close and lock an immense barred gate that would seal off that end of the corridor from the outer door.

Guns blasted deafeningly and the guards died with their mission unaccomplished. The bandits pounded through the narrow opening. On their right was a closed door of iron, masked with a sheathing of wood and bearing the words "Warden's Office". Indio skidded to a halt and rapped on the door.

From inside a heavy voice called, "Who is it? What's all the commotion about? What's going on out there?"

"Rodriguez, *senor,*" Indio called back in a meek, apologetic voice. He grinned and winked at Nino. "There was a little trouble, *senor,* but it is over now. I was told to report the matter to you."

After a moment, a small, square panel opened in the upper part of the door and the beefy face of the warden peered out. Indio smiled pleasantly and shot the warden between the eyes. A spring slammed the panel shut as he fell.

Indio stood facing the door, holding his smoking gun. His shoulders began to heave with ragged gasps. The smile on his face twisted into a mask of savage fury. Abruptly, he pushed the door panel open, reached through and emptied his gun into the body on the floor. Then, sagging against the door, he reloaded with shaking hands, plucking the bullets from Nino's bandolier.

Then they burst out and ran across the yard to the outer gate. As the bandits struggled to lift away the heavy bar, two more guards slammed into sight. Nino's gun thundered twice and the guards tumbled down like empty sacks, their lives seeping out into the thirsty dust.

As the gate swung open, Indio glimpsed a flicker of movement behind the little guard shanty. Gun in hand, he ran to the spot. A wounded guard, his eyes glazed with pain and fright, was huddled against the wall. Indio clawed a hard hand into the man's jacket and jerked him erect, a cocked pistol against the sagging head.

The bandit stared at the guard, his grin widening as the dark face sagged into hopeless resignation. Then abruptly Indio lowered his gun and sent the guard sprawling with a hard shove. "I am letting you live, hero. That is so you can spread the word of this day's doing. Tell everyone what you have seen take place here!"

He whirled and ran out to where Nino stood. "This way!" Nino gestured. "The horses are hidden close by in a small *orroyo*. We have brought your favourite for you."

As they swung into their saddles, Nino turned to his chief. "Where do we go first, *Senor* Indio?"

At the innocent question, Indio's grin faded and his face turned dark and twisted with savage hate. He snarled, "Is it necessary for you to ask, fool? Did you think the killing was ended when it has only begun?"

CHAPTER 5

THE house was a tiny, straw-thatched, one-room adobe, windowless and almost lost in the blazing immensity of the barren land. A single scrawny cottonwood drooped above the low roof, its leaves seared and withered by the blazing sun. In a patch of shade on the north side of the house, a pitiful scrap of garden struggled to survive. A few yards beyond, a thatched roof on poles served as a barn, offering meagre shelter to a lone horse, a handful of chickens and a rickety buckboard.

"It is not," Indio remarked, "a fit mansion for one so suddenly wealthy as our Tomaso, eh?"

The knot of outlaws swung down from their saddles into the smoking dust, dropping the reins to ground-halter their mounts. Indio led the way to the single closed door and knocked gently. It was opened by a woman, young and darkly pretty, with a chubby baby clutched by one arm.

At the sight of the callers her eyes flew wide and a scream of sheer terror tore from her throat. Indio sent her spinning aside with a sweep of his arm and tramped into the room, the others at his heels.

A slim, dark-skinned young man sprang up from a bench and froze, his mouth sagging open, his eyes wild with fright. "Mother of God," he mumbled. *"Indio!"*

"You did not expect to see me so soon, Tomaso?" Indio asked, his voice deceptively soft and pleasant. He took two quick steps and smashed his fist full into the ashen face. The man flew backward into the wall and down to his hands and knees, blood streaming from his nose.

Before he could move, two of Indio's men were upon him. One caught him by the hair and jerked his head back so hard that the grating of neck-bones was audible in the room. The other pulled the young man's hands behind his back and lashed them with a length of rawhide. They held him on his knees while the grinning Indio systematically pulped the upturned face with vicious open-hand slaps.

"For money," the bandit said softly, timing the words to the slaps. "For—lousy—*dinero.*"

The young woman came out of her first paralysis of terror and flung herself at Indio, trying to pull him away. "No! No! No! God of mercy, no!" she screamed. Two of Indio's men dragged her back and backed her against the wall, the baby, still in her arms, wailing with fright.

"You took money—blood money—to betray me, to put me in a cage like a wild animal." Indio leaned forward and spat into the bloody face. "You should have killed me when you could, Tomaso. It would have been much better for you . . ." He straightened and his smile was the face of all evil, ". . . and for *them.*"

Indio turned suddenly to the woman and the shrieking baby. From a vest pocket he got out a fat gold watch on the end of a chain. He touched a hidden knob, the watch case flew open and from within came the thin, sweet tinkle of tiny chimes. The baby stopped crying to stare in fascination at the strange, gleaming toy.

Indio smiled like a proud grandfather at the trembling woman. "How old is the boy?"

With an effort, she managed to choke out, "Eighteen months."

"Eighteen months," Indio repeated softly. "Well, well! Just the time I was caged in that prison cell." Abruptly and savagely, he whirled back to the kneeling Tomaso. "So you used the reward for my betrayal to start raising a family. I feel that, in a way, that makes your family partly mine." His smile became incredibly ugly. "I'll take my part now."

Indio jerked his head. Nino, seeming to have an uncanny ability to read his leader's thoughts and plans, took a spare pistol from his belt and tucked it into the kneeling man's empty holster. Straightening, Nino caught the whimpering woman by the wrist and half-dragged her out through the door into the blazing sunlight, the baby screaming on her arm.

The kneeling man struggled frantically against the restraining hands. He cried wildly, thickly, "Dear God, no! They are both innocent. Indio, you *know* they are innocent. I was the one who sold you out—the only one. In the name of the Virgin, show mercy to them and take your price from me."

As if not a word had reached his ears, his face blank, his eyes remote, Indio snapped open the watch again.

He stood with his head cocked, eyes half-closed, listening to the chimes, completely lost in the fragile melody.

Outside, the woman screamed once, her voice shrill above the wailing of the baby. Then two pistol shots slammed and there was only a terrible silence.

Indio snapped the watch-case shut, cutting off the tinkling melody. He studied the writhing, moaning figure on the floor.

"Now," the bandit said softly, "I think you hate me enough to make our last meeting truly . . . interesting."

At his gesture, Tomaso was jerked to his feet. Indio slowly stripped off his coat and tossed it to the floor. He held out a hand and one of his men hastily unbuckled his own gunbelt and handed it over. Indio put it on, grinning at the bloody figure opposite him.

"You are a fortunate man, Tomaso, for not many are given a second chance to correct a bad mistake. Your mistake was in not shooting me. For the sake of old times, *amigo,* I am giving you a second chance." To his men, Indio said, "Cut him loose."

A knife freed the bound wrists and the bandits stepped away, leaving the betrayer alone at the end of the room, with the loaded pistol sagging against his thigh in a bitter mockery of hope.

"Now we are ready," Indio said. He got out the gold watch and handed it to one of his men. "The music will play until the spring runs down. When the last chime sounds, we will begin." The bandit peered at his victim with mock anxiety. "Do you think you can? Your colour is not good, old friend. Are you sure you feel well enough?"

The blaze of hatred on the other's face sent Indio into a spasm of laughter. But he abruptly choked off. He nodded to his man. The watch snapped open and the chimes began again.

The sound ran on and on, while sweat mingled with the blood on Tomaso's battered face. It seemed an eternity until the music began to slow down, the intervals between the notes growing gradually longer. The final chime lingered and died into silence—a silence instantly broken by the slap of palms against walnut and steel.

Hate and desperation gave the doomed man superhuman speed in his draw, but not quite speed enough. The gunshots thundered almost in unison, but Tomaso's slug went into the dirt floor. He pitched forward, a bullet through his heart.

Indio dropped his gun into its holster and reached out to retrieve the watch. His whole body seemed to be wilting, shrinking in upon itself. His face was slack, his eyes muddy and empty. He pulled himself up with an effort and gestured sharply.

"Out! All of you. And take that with you."

The outlaws filed out silently, two of them carrying the dead man between them. Indio stumbled to the bench and sagged down on it, his breath coming in short, barking sobs.

After a few moments his breathing quieted. He put his head down on the rough wood of the table beside him. He was drained of the blood lust that had driven him, a killer satiated at last. Nino came in silently, rolling and moistening a brown paper cigarette. He put it between Indio's slack lips, struck a match to light it, then went out without speaking.

The cigarette burning down to his lips aroused Indio. He got up briskly, spitting out the stub, and strode outside like a man reborn. His band was waiting in the sparse shade of the withered tree.

"Mount up," Indio barked. "We ride to our headquarters now and send word to every man who ever rode with us to come at once. There are great plans to be made."

"You are planning something big, *amigo?*" Nino asked.

"Big?" Indio laughed wildly. "We are going to make a richer haul than you ever dreamed of—richer than any ever made by any *bandido* in all time, my friend."

CHAPTER 6

THE news of Indio's bloody breakout whipped through the territory like wildfire, carried by racing horsemen and chattering telegraph keys. With it went a wave of terror. Businessmen closed up shop or hired armed guards and carried on nervously surrounded by weapons. Ranchers stayed inside, behind barred doors to guard their families. Posses, armed to the teeth, fanned out across the countryside but took good care *not* to find the trail of the killers.

Almost before the bodies of the prison guards had been buried, printing presses were rolling out the posters, offering ten thousand dollars for Indio, dead or alive, and lesser amounts for his known accomplices. Every town for a hundred miles around rang with the sound of hammers nailing up the bounty notices. The bestial face of the killer, mouth open in mad laughter, looked down from every wall and post in the territory.

The sheriff of Los Gallos finished nailing up his last poster and trudged back to his tiny office and jail. At the door, he paused to look at a stranger riding into town from the north. He noted that the bearded rider was very tall, his lean figure draped in a brown-and-white poncho. His horse was a handsome bay with white stockings. The sheriff stared for a moment with mild curiosity, then shrugged and went on inside.

The Man With No Name spied the fresh whiteness of the new poster and swung out of the saddle. He looked first at the size of the reward and his eyes went wide. A spark began to glow in their depths and a smile of anticipation lifted the corners of his stern mouth.

He got out a stubby *cigarro,* lit it carefully and stood puffing it while he fixed every detail of the bandit's face in his mind. When it was indelibly printed in his memory, he took a step towards the door of the sheriff's office. Then, changing his mind, he led the bay down the dusty street toward a hitchrail where a dozen saddled horses stood in a close bunch. For a man trained to listen and weigh, there was no better place to pick up information than a crowded saloon.

Some forty miles away, Colonel Douglas Mortimer tied his big black to a hitchrail and walked toward a bright new poster. He had almost reached it when he stopped short, his body going rigid with shock. His burning gaze was fixed, not on the size of the bounty, but upon the laughing face of the wanted bandit.

It was the face that had driven him and haunted his nightmares through a black eternity.

The director of the bank frowned as he ran a finger down a page of an open ledger. He swung it around towards a waiting teller. "You'd better check those figures again. They don't look quite right to me."

"Yes, sir."

The director looked up as a tall man in a long frock coat approached the cage. He assessed the stranger's bearing and the obvious quality of his dress and was visibly impressed.

"Good afternoon, sir. May I be of service to you?"

"My name is Mortimer," the stranger said. "Douglas Mortimer."

"Oh, yes. Colonel Mortimer. Do come right in." The director unlocked the cage door, then locked it again behind his visitor. He gestured toward his private office behind the cage. "From Virginia, isn't it?"

"Carolina," the Colonel corrected.

"That's right, Carolina. A valued colleague wrote that you'd be in town and might call upon me to discuss a financial matter. Please be seated. Cigar, sir?"

The director started to sit down behind a big desk, then jumped up as a teller looked inquiringly in at the door. "Excuse me one moment, sir. Come right in, Harry."

The banker selected a key from a bunch he carried on a chain and used it to unlock a massive safe in the corner. He opened the door and stepped back to let the teller get a tray of gold pieces from inside. Then, locking the safe again, he returned to his chair.

"Now, what can I do to assist you, Colonel Mortimer?"

The Colonel had refused the cigar, lit his yellow meerschaum, blew out the match and leaned forward. "I'm looking for a first-class bank."

"Oh, but exactly, sir," the director said, beaming.

"The largest and most secure bank in the territory."

"Well, now, Colonel Mortimer, I want to assure you that our bank here has everything—all the safeguards you would expect for the protection of your money."

"I don't doubt that," the Colonel said, "but I might have an exceptionally large sum to deposit. Now, just suppose that I am a bandit . . ."

The director started violently and turned pale. "A *bandit?*" he bleated in a high voice. He swallowed hard and glanced nervously at the safe in the corner.

"A very dangerous bandit, sir, with a gang of dangerous killers who would stop at nothing." The Colonel paused to let the banker squirm. "Now, in such a case, what would be absolutely the most impossible bank in the entire territory for me to rob?"

The director's breath gusted out in a sigh of relief. "In such a case, the one bank I would suggest is the Bank of El Paso. Not even that terrible Indio and his pack of murderers would dare to attack that one. Why, it's more than a bank, sir. It is a fortress—an impregnable fortress."

The Colonel got to his feet. "I believe there is still time for me to catch the train to El Paso." He extended his hand. "Thank you for your help. You've told me exactly what I wanted to know."

The banker pumped the Colonel's strong paw in obvious relief. "A pleasure to be of service, Colonel Mortimer. I will telegraph my colleague at the Bank of El Paso that you will be calling upon him."

The Man With No Name rode into El Paso under a bright morning sun. It was bigger than the towns he had known, the buildings higher and more solid, but at this hour the wide main street was practically empty.

A group of brown-skinned urchins were pitching horseshoes in the dust. One, a bright-eyed boy of perhaps twelve, detached himself and ran toward the new arrival, shouting, "Hey, mister, Captain, General, welcome to El Paso. Do you need a stable for your fine horse? Or a room, perhaps? Maybe you want to take a nice bath? My name is Fernando. The stable is right here and that is your hotel there on the corner just beyond it."

The bounty hunter studied the street silently. Diagonally across from the indicated hotel was another, also on the corner. He looked down. "Why this hotel and not that one over there?"

The boy made a grimace of distaste. "You wouldn't like that other one, *Senor*. You would not like it one bit. You'd have to stay up half the night shooting cockroaches to keep them from eating up your boots."

"Is that so?" the hunter asked solemnly.

"At this hotel the room will cost you much less."

"Besides," the man on the bay horse said, "this one pays you better for steering guests to them."

"Whatever you say, *senor,*" the boy grinned, unabashed. His voice became confidential. "Besides, this hotel has a land*lady,* and she is not old."

The tall man raised his eyebrows. "Married?"

"Oh, yes. But she does not let this interfere with making her guests—er—comfortable."

The bounty hunter swung down, took his saddlebags and slung them over his left shoulder. He handed the reins to Fernando. "Tell them a thorough rubdown and to go light on the oats."

He stood looking at a building opposite the hotel. It was a large, square structure of whitewashed stucco, its front door and windows covered with heavy iron bars. It could easily be mistaken for a prison, and a formidable one, but for the sign above the door: "Bank Of El Paso."

Fernando suddenly materialised at the bounty hunter's elbow. "That is the bank, *senor*. It is where I am going to put my money." He slanted a sharp-eyed look at the tall man and added, suggestively, "As soon as I get some money to put in, that is."

The hunter studied the boy thoughtfully, then dug under the poncho and brought out a shiny new fifty-cent piece. He flipped it enticingly, watching the wise young eyes light up. "To get money to put in the bank, Fernando, you first have to earn it. Now you could earn this half-dollar easily."

Fernando leaned close and whispered hoarsely, "Who you want killed, General?"

A fleeting grin touched the stern lips. "All you have to do is let me know immediately when you spot a stranger in town, someone you've never seen around El Paso before."

The boy's hand darted out and snatched the spinning coin. "Look across the street, in front of that other hotel," he said.

The hunter turned his head slowly. A tall man in a long frock coat was standing at the edge of the boardwalk, looking up and down the street, his manner that of a stranger taking his bearings. After a moment he turned and went off down the street, his tall figure stiffly erect, his stride that of one who has spent much of his life marching to bugles and drums.

The hunter frowned. "Where's he staying?"

Fernando made an elaborate pretence of not hearing. He began humming, tossing the fifty-cent piece in the air.

"I get it," the hunter said. He fished out another coin. *"Bandido!"*

Fernando grinned. "At that hotel. Now you will want me to tell you in which room." He caught a glint in the tall man's narrowed eyes and his grin faded. He said hastily, "This will cost you nothing, *senor*. Upstairs—the middle window on the front, just over the front door."

"Keep watching," the bounty hunter said and turned to his own hotel door, his face like chiselled granite. It was not Fernando's small greed that had brought the glitter into his eyes; it was the sudden thought that had struck him as the boy spoke.

It might be only coincidence, of course, but the other man's window looked almost directly down on to the front door of the bank. The stranger who occupied that room would bear watching.

A woman with a lush figure and a mass of copper-red hair was behind the small desk of the hotel, entering figures in a dog-eared ledger. The neckline of her dark silk dress was scooped so low that, as she bent over the page, her full bosom seemed in imminent danger of bursting out completely.

The bounty hunter came in so soundlessly that she was unaware of his presence until he rang the bell at her elbow. She jumped and a small, moon-faced man with steel-rimmed glasses popped up from somewhere behind the desk, clutching a pewter pot and a cleaning rag. He looked at the newcomer with faint distaste.

"Help you, sir?" It was quite obvious that he hoped the answer would be "no."

"Yes," the hunter said coldly. "I want the room that's located right above your desk."

"I'm sorry," the proprietor said, looking glad. "That room happens to be occupied. In fact, the entire hotel is filled to capacity at the moment. It's too bad. But the room you want happens to be our best and it's always occupied."

The hunter stared at him, the narrowed eyes cold and unwinking. "By who?"

The proprietor's washed-out eyes shifted behind his glasses. "Mary, check the register."

The woman had been staring at the tall stranger with open interest. She turned reluctantly and got a thick book from a lower shelf, taking plenty of time to give the newcomer the full effect of her scooped-out neckline and deep cleavage. She straightened and opened the register. "That is *Senor* Martinez."

"You see," the proprietor sneered triumphantly. "I told you it is occupied—by *Senor* Martinez. I am sorry."

The hunter reached over, plucked the register out of the woman's hands and spun it around. He took the wooden desk pen from its inkwell and drew a thick line across the entry.

"It's free now—or will be when I take care of it."

The proprietor's moon face turned dark. "That room is taken."

"I know," the tall man said quietly. "That's what I've been trying to tell you."

He hoisted the saddlebags higher on his shoulder and tramped the stairs leading upward beyond the desk. The proprietor pounded the desk in helpless rage. "He's nothing but an animal—a wild, vicious animal."

His wife sighed dreamily. "But so tall, and so good looking. And those powerful arms that could crush a woman." She shot her husband a look of deepest loathing. "He would make love like a man—a real man."

"You're just *dirty,*" he spat.

From overhead came a sharp commotion—the scraping of feet, the crash of an overturned chair, a man's sharp yelp of pain or terror. There was a pounding of running feet and then a swarthy, thickset man burst down the stairs with shirt tails flying. As he ran, he was trying to jam an armload of clothing into an open carpet bag.

He fell against the desk, panting. "Proprietor! Quick, my bill! I want my bill. Before *he* comes down here, give me my bill."

The moon-faced hotelman held up placating hands. "Now, now, Mr. Martinez, there is no need for you to check out. The sheriff will be back in town tomorrow and I will see that he takes care of that . . ."

"My bill!" the swarthy man repeated, almost in tears. "I must check out at once. I cannot stay a minute longer." He flung an appealing hand toward

the woman. "Mary, you give me my bill. He does not understand."

"But Mr. Martinez," the hotelman insisted, "I assure you everything is going to be all right. You won't be bothered by him again, I promise you. I'll give you another room immediately, the best in the house. We'll give Mr. Martinez the bridal suite, won't we, Mary?"

Martinez hammered the desk with clenched fists. "I want my bill, not more talk. Can't you understand? I would like to stay but it is not possible, I have to get out of this town immediately. I have remembered a most important appointment elsewhere, a very long way from here."

"*Senor* Martinez."

The swarthy man whirled, saw the tall, ponchoed figure on the stairs and sagged against the desk, his knees wobbling.

"Y-yes, *senor*? Wh-what is it you w-want of me now?"

"Here." The hunter tossed down a pair of flannel long johns. "I don't wear 'em."

Martinez snatched them up, babbling with relief. "Oh, I am honoured that you thought of me. Oh, thank you, thank you . . ."

The hunter bolted the door of his hotel room, got a folded paper from his saddlebag and lay back on the bed. He opened the paper to reveal the reward poster on Indio, studying the brutish face fondly.

"You sweetheart," he murmured softly. "You

beautiful, beautiful beast. Ten thousand dollars riding on one little slug of lead. Baby, you're going to give me what I've been chasing all these years, and God help any man who tries to get between us and pick you off for himself."

In the centre room of the hotel across the street, Colonel Douglas Mortimer sat in his shirt sleeves, painstakingly cleaning and oiling his deadly guns.

CHAPTER 7

UNLIKE the hideout of the run-of-the-mill outlaw chief, the headquarters of the dread Indio was no carefully hidden cave to be searched out at the risk of slow and agonizing death. Any man in the territory could, in fact, point out the place—but only from a very great distance. No one in his right mind would get within gunshot, and only a posse determined on mass suicide would be so reckless as to storm its walls.

The big adobe building had been an important mission since the days of those other ruthless marauders, the *Conquistadores.* Indio and his band had taken it over by the simple device of slaughtering its gentle and defenceless occupants and dragging their bodies out to be disposed of by four-legged wolves. The large chapel which occupied the main floor became dining hall, meeting room and site of orgies for the bandits. The sparsely furnished cells upstairs served as their sleeping quarters.

On this day, the chapel was crowded with the most vicious pack of killers to assemble there since the days of Spain's glory. More than thirty of Indio's most trusted companions were already assembled and others were on the way.

The huge centre table held a large hunk of half-raw beef and chunks of bread. There were no utensils or dishes. The bandits used their hunting knives to hack off great pieces of meat and wolfed them down with draughts of wine. There was a deafening babble of coarse talk and laughter as the men bragged of plunder they had seized, of victims they had murdered, of exquisite new tortures they had devised and of women they had raped and killed.

As always with rough men, there was violent horse-play. A bandit drew his knife and winked at a companion. "Watch this." The knife whipped across the room and thudded into the back of a massive oak chair, a scant inch from the throat of the outlaw occupying it. The man choked on a chunk of bread, cursed wildly and jumped to his feet. Jerking out the knife, he leaped towards the thrower, only to be tripped and disarmed by guffawing onlookers.

Indio sat apart from his beast-pack, ignoring the uproar. He was fanning himself, eyes half-closed, lost in private thoughts of his own. He sat up, instantly alert, as hoofbeats pounded into the churchyard. Spurs jingled and a swarthy man tramped in, grinning, lifting an arm in salute.

"Hello, my friends. Hello, Indio. It is good to have you free and back in business again. You can see I didn't waste a minute getting here, Indio calls and Groggy comes running."

He tore off a great chunk of bread and stuffed it into his mouth. Indio looked from the newcomer to the door and frowned.

"Where is Sancho? He was to come with you."

Groggy swallowed with painful effort and spread his

hands. "If you are waiting for Sancho, I might as well go home again and come back in about four years, *amigo*. That is when they will let Sancho out of prison. Poor fellow, four years with no *dinero,* no *amor*. Bad for him—not so bad for the rest of us. A man who gets caught doesn't deserve either respect or a share of the loot, eh?" He hauled a stool around and sat down, facing Indio. "Now, what's this all about, huh?"

The chieftain got to his feet. "Listen carefully, all of you." He unfolded the paper he had taken from his dead cellmate at the prison and displayed a crudely drawn map. "This, my friends, is the inside layout of the Bank of El Paso, the strongest and richest bank in the territory."

He frowned at the map, then around the room. "We'll say this room is the inside of the bank. Over there, where Nino stands, would be the bank safe."

Groggy snorted and spat on the floor. "Which I happen to know weighs three tons and can't even be dented by a stick of dynamite."

Indio nodded absently and moved around the room, pointing. "Right here would be the room where the two cashiers are. Here is the manager's desk. Right behind him is a fancy cabinet filled with bottles of fine liquor for serving drinks to rich depositors. Over there is the main door, and directly opposite they built a double wall." He turned abruptly. "So what happens now, Groggy? Let's say you have killed the two cashiers and the manager. For the next few minutes you are the boss of the whole bank. So what now, my big brain?"

"Now," Groggy said disgustedly, "I find out quick I have wasted three good bullets and my time because I still can't get at the money."

Indio nodded. "Exactly, my friend. A complete waste of time. Because, Groggy, to blast open that damn iron safe, we'd have to be using so much dynamite that the whole bank would just disappear—and we'd all go up with it." A wolfish grin spread over Indio's face. "And even if we got it open, we might discover that the presence of a safe doesn't necessarily signify that there is money inside."

He grinned at the blank, puzzled expressions on the circle of savage faces. "You think all this makes no sense, eh? You think maybe Indio left his wits back in that prison cell?"

Chuckling, he went to a stairway leading up to a small balcony from which priests had once held mass. "To help you understand my meaning, I would like to tell you a nice little story—what church people call a parable."

Indio put his hands on the balcony railing and looked down at the upturned faces. "Once upon a time there was a carpenter. You don't think a carpenter could make much money, eh? No? But you're wrong. This one did because he was a builder of very fine cabinets. So one day a banker decides that he must fool honest bandits like ourselves and have his iron safe disguised as a fine wood cabinet.

"To get it made, the banker seeks out this carpenter of whom he has heard much, but . . ." Indio paused, holding up a finger, letting his men's curiosity build up. ". . . He does not tell our carpenter who he is or the name of the bank."

They were beginning to catch on now. Several of the less stupid licked their lips and a glitter of anticipation and greed lit their eyes. Indio let the silence build, savouring his climax.

"One day the carpenter just happens to be in El Paso and happens to go into the bank. Inside, behind many barred doors, he sees the big safe that weighs, as Groggy says, three tons and resists dynamite. Then, behold, over against another wall looking innocent as can be, stands the very cabinet he himself had built to disguise a safe. Then he knew where the Bank of El Paso *really* keeps its money—more than a million dollars."

There was a collective gasp. Then wild cheering and a gust of gleeful laughter. Bandits whooped and pounded one another's backs and some did little dances of joy. Indio lifted his hands for silence.

"You think that carpenter was a lucky man, the way things worked out to have him build that secret safe, then walk into the very bank where it stands. Sad to say, it was not true. Because, while he was dreaming and scheming and drawing plans, he made a little mistake and got sent to prison. There, poor fellow, he was put in the same cell with a prisoner named Indio. And he talked often in his sleep, and when he thought Indio was not awake, he worked on a perfect little model of the safe-cabinet."

Indio reached under his jacket and brought out the small white brick-sized object he had snatched from his cell mate. He tossed it down to Groggy. "Study every detail most thoroughly, then pass it around. I want every one of you to be able to recognize the real safe without a mistake or an instant's hesitation. When you are finished, we will sit down and I will tell all my plans."

Indio had gone over every detail of the plan in his mind, going over it and over it, refining every step, anticipating every conceivable obstacle. There was only one small disappointment to mar his satisfaction. If everything went according to plan, there would be only a handful of persons to kill.

Still, there would be the one great consolation. Indio shook his head slowly at the wonder of it and whispered softly to himself, "Not even Indio has ever stolen a million dollars all at one time before."

CHAPTER 8

THE director of the Bank of El Paso had yet to see one penny of the enormous wealth the strange man kept talking about. Nevertheless, he was sufficiently impressed by the stranger's bearing and obviously expensive tailoring to accord him a rare honour. From a carved cabinet he brought out two glasses and a bottle reserved for only the wealthiest depositors.

The director carefully poured out two glasses and put the bottle away before seating himself. "Now, Mr. Mortimer, how can we be of service to you?"

The Colonel finished lighting his pipe and blew out the match with a cloud of fragrant blue smoke. "Your colleague in Tucumcari assures me that your bank has the largest deposits in the entire territory."

"That is absolutely corect, Mr. Mortimer. Here at the Bank of El Paso, we maintain a constant cash reserve of, well, let us just say, considerably more than a half-million dollars."

The Colonel's soundless whistle indicated the proper respect. "Then you must be very certain that your bank is amply secure to safeguard such a large sum."

"Certain indeed," the director said, smiling. "From the moment your money is on deposit here, you may sleep at night in perfect confidence and without a shadow of worry."

The banker waved his hand towards a series of barred doors that separated each department from the other as well as from his own office where the gigantic three-ton safe stood so convincingly. The Colonel, who had already fixed every detail in his mind, nodded with the air of a man deeply impressed.

"In addition, sir, when the bank is closed, an armed guard always remains here, in front of the vault, while two armed patrols constantly circle the outside of the building. In addition to all this," the director dropped his voice to a conspiratorial whisper, "we have taken certain other precautions which are known only to myself and another officer."

"My, my," the Colonel said, shaking his head in admiration, "not even the Bank of San Francisco is this well protected."

"Precisely, sir. The truth is, Mr. Mortimer, that to try robbing us in any manner would be so futile that only a complete and utter fool would attempt it."

The Colonel nodded. "Or a complete madman," he murmured softly.

To a bounty hunter, patience was the most basic of tools. But when the waiting was coupled with a small and nagging uncertainty, it began to claw at even the most iron nerves.

The Man With No Name was almost positive that he had considered every angle and reached the only possible conclusion as to what the next step in the grim game would be. He was *almost* positive, but never quite. A madman can never be trusted to do the predictable, and Indio was undeniably mad. But he was also a creature of enormous greed, with an ego that must feed itself by accomplishing the impossible. This was the foundation of the hunter's careful planning.

But as the days dragged by with none of the anticipated moves taking place, the self-doubt grew. The Man With No Name was further irritated and puzzled by the fact that the tall, frock-coated stranger was still in El Paso and quite obviously also waiting for some person or event.

Except for occasional brief, aimless walks, the frock-coated man spent most of his time at the window of his hotel room, peering through a slit in the curtains at the traffic on the street or at the customers entering and leaving the bank. Several times the hunter had glimpsed a flash of light that might have been reflected from the lens of a telescope.

The hunter was lying on his bed, staring at the ceiling and reviewing every step of his plan when a shrill whistle sounded outside. He sprang up and ran to the open window. Fernando was in the street below, beckoning furiously. The Man With No Name whirled and ran out the door.

Downstairs, the red-haired Mary heard his step and put on her most inviting and seductive smile. She gave the front of her dress a tug to bare another alluring inch of cleavage. But the hunter shot by and out the front door without even a glance in her direction. She stamped a furious foot and stuck her tongue out at the closing door.

Fernando was waiting, suggestively flipping a coin.

The Man With No Name got a half-dollar from under his poncho and tossed it over. "You have news for me at last? Another stranger has come to town?"

Fernando nodded, then a crafty expression slid over his face. "Only minutes ago, *senor*. But I also have other news you will find well worth the small price."

The hunter snatched out a second coin. "Out with it, you rascal."

"There was a second stranger who rode in with the other. And there is still other news I might tell for a price."

A hard hand suddenly caught the front of Fernando's shirt and shook the boy violently. Narrowed eyes blazed into the small face. "You little devil! I'm all through playing games with you. I want to know how many strangers arrived altogether. Spit it out fast before I shake the news out of your grubby hide."

"Y-yes, sir, G-general, s-sir. First there were two who came riding in. Very rough, very mean." The boy's voice dropped to an imitation of a harsh snarl. " 'Get the hell out of our way, you stinkin' brats!' Then behind them came two more, just as mean and ugly."

"Where are they now?"

"Over there, across the street, *senor*. In the saloon of that other hotel."

The bounty hunter released the boy and went across the street, half running. This could be the pay-off on his greatest gamble, the confirmation of everything he had anticipated. If so, the waiting was over and now the action would begin.

He looked in over the low, swinging doors and saw the four men. They were drinking at the bar, crowded close together, their backs to him. He noted that each held his drink in the left hand and let the right dangle, always close to the gun in his tied-down holster. Three were big men, the fourth an under-sized hunchback who would probably be the most dangerous of all.

The hunter pushed through the doors and stopped by a supporting pillar, watching the four drinkers while he got out a *cigarro* and a match. As he struck a light, two of the men turned far enough for him to see their faces. The last lingering doubt vanished in a wave of elation.

He recognised them instantly from the bounty posters he had studied. Both were members of Indio's pack, with prices on their heads. The hunchback, then, would be the one whose unpredictable rages had earned the name of the Wild One. Altogether, the four would net him a tidy reward, but now he was after bigger game and they were more valuable to him alive than dead.

A movement drew the hunter's eyes to the staircase beside the bar. The stranger in the frock coat was coming down from his hotel room above, putting tobacco into a yellow pipe. The stranger glanced down at the four drinkers and the tawny eyes glittered with recognition. Recognition and something more that could have been elation.

The hunter froze in his place by the pillar. That fleeting blaze of expression had confirmed what had previously been only a dark suspicion. The stranger was a rival bounty killer. Worse, he was clearly stalking the same quarry.

The Colonel came past the four gun-slicks, holding a match and looking around for a spot to strike it. Then, calmly, he reached over and scratched it on the hunchback's suspender.

The four spun around, their faces slack with stunned incredulity. The bartender yelped and dived from sight behind the bar. A man dropped his whisky glass and scrambled wildly out of the line of fire.

The dumbfounded expression on the Wild One's face faded and hot fury blazed up in his pale blue eyes. A muscle twitched in his sallow cheek. As the Colonel coolly lifted the match to his pipe, the hunchback blew out the flame.

The Colonel examined the burned match thoughtfully, then let it drop. He reached out, grabbed the glowing cigar in the Wild One's hand and used its fiery end to light his pipe. The hunchback grimaced in wordless rage and snatched at his gun. But one of his companions grabbed the thin wrist, pinning the gun in its holster, muttering an inaudible warning in the Wild One's ear.

Shaking with suppressed fury, the hunchback reluctantly let go of his gun and began to back away. The Colonel gravely held out the cigar. The Wild One snarled and turned away; then all four men backed past the watching bounty hunter and out through the swinging doors.

The Colonel looked at the smoking cigar, shrugged and dropped it into a spittoon. He rapped on the bar.

"Whisky, please."

The bartender's pallid face lifted cautiously. "Mister, why in hell do you have to pick my place to try to commit suicide? Maybe you don't know that fellow, but I do and I can tell you it's nothin' but a miracle that you're standing there, still alive."

"Is that so? Now, why do you suppose a man would walk around, wearing a pistol with the holster tied down for action and let himself be openly insulted? Doesn't that seem mighty strange to you?"

The bartender finished pouring and bent forward. "Listen, mister, if that hunchback didn't kill you right then and there, it was because he had a very, very important reason for not starting a ruckus, and you can bet your boots on that."

"You know, friend," Colonel Douglas Mortimer said, as if the idea had never occurred to him, "you may be absolutely right."

He downed his drink and went back up the stairs toward his room.

The Man With No Name turned and pushed out through the saloon's door. The four gun-toughs were nowhere in sight, but the four strange horses that had been at the saloon hitchrail when Fernando summoned him were still there. He went up to his room, moving fast, his face grim. Things were breaking fast and his window was the best place to keep an eye on both the developing action and his dangerous rival.

He reached his post just in time to witness a daily tableau. Five men, wearing pistols and carrying rifles, stood in front of the bank, waiting. In a moment, the bank's director ushered out the last customers. The director waited for the inside guard to enter the building, then closed and locked the massive iron door. He nodded to the remaining four guards and went off briskly down the street.

The four men separated into two pairs, going in opposite directions for their all-night patrol circuit around and around the bank. Watching their steady tramping pace, the hunter suddenly spied the Wild One.

The hunchback was leaning against a hitchrail, watching the pair of patrolling guards on his side of the bank. His left hand was unconsciously tapping his thigh in perfect unison with their marching steps.

"Counting," the hunter muttered softly. "Timing their circuit and fixing the exact distance by the number of paces to a side."

Now that he understood exactly what the bandits were doing he had no trouble spotting two more of the outlaws. Each was lounging inconspicuously at a point where he could cover a different side of the bank. The fourth bandit was undoubtedly watching the far side from a spot beyond the hunter's line of vision. After following a few circuits by the guards, the four would have their movements timed to the split second.

The hunter looked across, then, at his rival's window. The eye of a small, brass-bound telescope peeped from between the curtains, moving steadily to follow the marching patrols. The hunter's face went hard and cold and his fingertips caressed the solid bulge of the gun beneath the poncho.

"Indio's *mine,* goddam you!" he muttered fiercely. "All mine."

With a sudden start, he realised that the eye of the telescope had swung and was staring straight at him.

CHAPTER 9

COLONEL DOUGLAS MORTIMER put the telescope down on the battered bureau beside the window and stood for a long time, staring thoughtfully into space. Finally he nodded, as if reaching a conclusion. He put on his frock coat, took his hat and went down to the street.

At the local newspaper office, the staff was happy to let him browse through its collection of small weeklies from towns throughout the territory. It took the Colonel only a very short while to come upon the item he was seeking.

BOUNTY KILLER GETS HIS MEN

The Marton Brothers, long wanted for a variety of vicious crimes, were out-gunned and slain on the street last night by a lone bounty hunter. Onlookers swear the Martons had their own guns clear of their holsters before their nemesis drew his from beneath a brown poncho with fantastic speed. Fanning the hammer, he killed them all before they could get off a single shot. In collecting the rich bounty, the killer flatly refused to tell either his name or where he came from. He was listed on the sheriff's record as "Man from nowhere with no name."

The Colonel strolled back to the hotel dining room and ate a leisurely if unappetizing supper. Afterward, he dawdled for some time over a drink. For the first time in many years he felt relaxed and at peace. With the end of the dark trail at last in sight, his nights were no longer haunted by the nightmare face of his quarry.

The only small cloud in his tranquil sky was the presence of a rival bounty hunter, quite obviously on a collision course towards the same prize. But even that was only a minor problem. If competition threatened to interfere with his purpose, then competition would be swiftly eliminated. He had yet to meet or hear of a man who could match his own lightning draw or deadly marksmanship.

The Colonel lit his pipe and went up to his room. He was in the act of laying out his gun-cleaning equipment when he was struck by a thought. He went to the window and looked across the dark street. There was no light in his rival's room. He stood for some time, frowning, staring across at the dark rectangle of the window.

The boy, Fernando, looked up sharply as a shadow fell across his feet. Then his look of alarm faded as he saw the coin in the hunter's hand. He scrambled and caught it deftly.

"That stranger who came just before me. The tall man in the long coat. I want to know his name, where he came from and what his business here is."

"That will not be easy, *senor*. Like you, he did not sign his name on the hotel register and he does not make conversation with others. I hear many men ask the same questions from curiosity but none can give the answers."

"There's got to be somebody who can tell me."

Fernando scratched his head, frowned, then brightened. "You could ask the Prophet."

"The *who*?"

"The prophet, *senor*. He is a very old man who lives in a shack by the railroad tracks. Long ago he used to tell fortunes but no longer. But they say he knows every man who ever wore a gun in the territory. I will show you his place."

A thin, cracked voice called, "Come in," at the bounty hunter's knock. He went into a dingy, littered room, lit by a smoky oil lamp. An incredibly withered old man with an unkempt tangle of hair and beard lay on a dirty bed. A sheet was pulled up to his chest but his booted feet stuck out at the bottom. He peered at his visitor with rheumy eyes, then jerked the sheet over his face.

"No, no, no, no! Go 'way! I know what you are. You're a bounty killer and I want no truck with killers. Git out!"

"Who told you about me?"

"I didn't have to have nobody tell me nothin'," the muffled voice cackled. "I know things—things other fellers don't know 'cause I'm the Prophet."

"Then," the hunter said patiently, hooking a chair around beside the bed, "you're just the one to tell what I want to know about another man." He described the Colonel's dress and bearing in minute detail.

When he finished, the old man bleated, "I don't

know 'im! I don't know 'im! I don't know 'im! I don't know nobody any more. I'm dead, do you understand." He jerked the sheet down and cackled at his visitor in a senile glee. "There was a time I knowed everybody, but that was a long while ago, when all this was prairie. But these days ever'body's in a hurry. It's your damn good-for-nothin' trains, that's why. Your damn trains—toot, toot, toot, ding, ding." He spat noisily at the wall. "Damn trains!"

The hunter sighed and took off his hat. He looked around for a place to put it, then hung it on the old man's boot. He settled back to wait out the garrulous old character with the infinite patience of his trade.

The Prophet sat up. "You know what they done to me? A feller come around from the railroad and says to me, 'Prophet, we got to run a train right through here so you got to sell us your land, or we'll hafta buy Baker's next door.' Well, sir, I told right out where he could put his damn railroad and he didn't like it one bit. So do you know what the sonuvabitch done to get even with me?"

He was interrupted by the scream of a whistle and the rising pound of drivers. A train thundered past so close that the wind of its passage rocked the shanty and a cloud of smoke and vented steam poured through the window. As the uproar faded into the distance, the old man asked again, "Yuh know what he done to me—him and his goddam trains?"

"I have a sort of idea," the hunter said. He put on his hat and got to his feet. "But I didn't come here to listen to you rattle on all night about trains. It's pretty obvious that you don't know anything . . ."

"You don't have to git insulting," the Prophet shrilled. "If that's all you come fer, you kin git to hell out of my house right now. Go on! Clear out afore I lose my temper . . . Now where in hell you think you're goin', boy?"

At the door, the hunter said, "Why, I thought I'd better leave before you went and lost that temper."

"God dang yuh, what's the matter with yuh? How can yuh be so God dang stupid, boy? Fetch me over that gun—the one hangin' on the wall there right behind you. Hurry it up."

The hunter took down the pistol, saw that it was empty and tossed it over. The old man gripped it for a moment and his faded eyes brightened. He put the gun across his middle, holding it angled in front of his left hip.

"That feller you was askin' about—does he wear his gun over here, like this, for a cross-belly grab?"

"That he does, old-timer."

"Well, why in hell didn't yuh say so in the first place, yuh idjit? O' course I know the man you mean. He's Colonel Douglas Mortimer, a brave man and a fine soldier once. He used to be knowed as the best shot in the Carolinas."

"Colonel Douglas Mortimer," the hunter repeated softly.

"One day he jest up an' left the Army to become a bounty killer like you. Nobody knowed why, but I coulda told 'em. It was them trains, them goddam tootin' trains that done it."

The hunter dropped a banknote on the grimy bed and went out. Now, at least, he knew the identity of the rival he would kill, if necessary, to achieve his own purpose.

As he came past the depot he saw that the ticket window was open, the agent lounging expectantly at the counter. A fleeting grin touched the bounty hunter's lips as he turned and walked up to the window.

"There a train out from El Paso tonight?"

"It depends on which way you aim to go, mister."

"Anywhere. Just out."

"Yeah. There'll be one goin' to Santa Fe in about half an hour if it don't hit another cow and jump the track again."

"That'll do just fine, friend," the hunter said. "Don't close up because there'll be a passenger coming along right shortly to buy a ticket."

He turned and strode purposely off into the night.

Colonel Mortimer finished polishing the long pistol and slicking the inside of its holster with beeswax. He tested its draw and nodded with satisfaction. He looked across and saw that there was still no lamplight in his rival's room. Frowning he got his hat and started towards the door.

With his hand on the knob he hesitated, reconsidering his impulse and deciding against it. He took off his hat again and tossed it on the bed in case he changed his mind. He was in the act of taking off his long coat when the door opened. His hand whipped to his gun, then fell away, while an expression of utter astonishment froze on his face.

A small, wrinkled Chinese in coolie pyjamas and a pillbox hat came silently in. Without so much as a glance at the gaping man, he padded across to the closet, got out the Colonel's empty valise and opened it on the bed. He went to the bureau, got out the Colonel's spare clothing and equipment and wordlessly packed it into the bag. Still without glancing toward the stunned watcher, he closed the valise, picked it up and trotted out the door.

The Colonel snatched his hat and followed, down the stairs and out into the dark street. The bounty hunter in the brown poncho stood just beyond the boardwalk, his feet planted apart in the dust, hands close to his sides. His face was like a mask that might have been chiselled in granite.

He jerked his head at the Chinese. "Take it to the depot. The gentleman is leaving on the night train."

The coolie had only taken two steps before the Colonel came out of his daze and barked, "Take the bag back to the gentleman's room. The gentleman is not leaving on any train."

Obediently, the Chinese turned back towards the hotel door. The hunter rasped, "I'm giving the orders. To the depot."

"To my room," the Colonel roared.

The Chinese uttered a piercing shriek and dropped the valise, which flew open, spilling shirts and underwear. The man ran off down the street, waving his arms and yelling.

The Colonel walked a few slow steps and stepped off

the walk to face his rival. They stood for a long moment, almost chest-to-chest, each taking the other's measure in silence. When his steady glare failed to make the other blink or shift his eyes, the hunter looked down at the Colonel's elegant boots, polished to a dazzling shine. Slowly and deliberately, he tramped his own dusty boot down on the gleaming leather and ground it savagely, watching the pale brown eyes for a hint of reaction.

When the hunter lifted his boot, a broad smear of dirt marred the high lustre. The Colonel studied the blemish thoughtfully for a time. Then, with equal deliberation, he tramped down hard on the hunter's foot, grinding his own boot into it.

Without warning the hunter brought up his fist in a hard, sledging right to the other's jaw. The Colonel flew backward, landing on his shoulders in a cloud of dust. After a moment he got to his feet, moving slowly and carefully, watching the expressionless granite face.

He dusted himself off, then reached down to retrieve his fallen hat. His fingers were on it when his adversary's hand whipped under the poncho and out with lightning speed. The hunter's gun slammed and the Colonel's hat flew out of its owners grasp, coming to rest a dozen paces down the street.

Colonel Mortimer backed carefully to where the hat rested and reached again. Again the gun thundered and the headpiece flew down the street. The shots came steadily until the hunter's gun was empty and his rival far down the street. The Man With No Name shook out the empty shells and reloaded while the

Colonel picked up the riddled hat, dusted it and settled it back on his head.

The reloading finished, the gun lifted and thundered twice. Two spurts of dust geysered up between the Colonel's feet. The hunter lowered his gun to his side then, and stood, silent and watchful.

Without haste the Colonel drew his own gun. Taking his time with the aim, he fired. The other's hat flew from his head and high into the air. As it came down, another shot sent it spinning up again. It settled to the street only when the long-barrelled pistol was empty.

The Colonel tramped forward, reloading as he walked, until he faced his adversary. He snapped the cylinder closed and slid the weapon back into its holster.

"I'd call it just about a draw," he said. "There's a bottle of pretty good whisky upstairs that your Chinaman overlooked."

After a moment, the hunter said, "I'll help you gather up your belongings."

While the Colonel poured the drinks, the hunter sat by the table, examining the long-barrelled pistol and its detached stock. He fitted the two together, shaking his head. "How can anybody in our business go around lugging a contraption like this?"

"That contraption, as you call it," the Colonel said dryly, "could have sent you to your grave."

"Don't forget, Colonel, I was only shooting at your hat."

"And I was only shooting at yours." After a moment

he added softly, "*This* time."

They lifted their glasses in a wordless toast and sipped appreciatively. The Colonel studied his young rival. "Boy, I've managed to stay alive almost fifty years with my system, and I expect to be around for a few more. Not many men last that long around these parts. How long do you think you can last?"

"A lot longer than that, Colonel. There's a nice little spread upcountry that I've had my sights on for a long, long time. When I get my hands on Indio and that ten thousand dollars, I'll be able to buy it and hang up my gun for good."

"It's important to have your sights on a goal," the Colonel said. "I don't want to touch off another fight, but I feel I ought to remind you of one little point you seem to be overlooking, son."

"Yeah? And what's that?"

"I'm out to get Indio myself."

"Sure, and you're welcome to him—after me."

"Or before you," the Colonel said. He finished packing the yellow meerschaum and added quietly, "Or we get him together."

The hunter looked up sharply. "Is that a proposition?"

"Uh-huh." The Colonel sucked fire into his pipe and blew out the match. "An equal partnership. We split the risk and the money right down the middle."

"Why? Why should I split anything with anybody? I've done all right so far playing it alone."

"Well, offhand I can think of three mighty good reasons, my boy. The first one is the odds. Just counting the men he keeps close to him all the time, the ones he comes closest to trusting, there are fourteen pretty fast guns to buck. That's a lot for any man—or even two men."

"Yeah, Colonel. But it's also a lot of *dinero* for me if I bring it off by myself. Don't forget there's a bounty on every one of those others, too. What's your second good reason?"

"If we don't team up, those odds jump to fifteen to one."

"I don't get it," the hunter said harshly. "Are you saying if I don't buy your deal, you'll throw in with Indio?"

"You aren't using your head, boy," the Colonel said sadly. "Look, when two hunters go after the same prey and they're both desperate, one of them is apt to get a mite careless and shoot the other in the back. If that should happen in this case, it would only benefit Indio."

"And the third reason?"

"We've each worked out a plan of some kind that we're keeping to ourselves. If we try to go our separate ways, my plan could easily wreck yours and get you killed, or the other way around. By the way, I'm curious about one thing. How did you come to pick the Bank Of El Paso as Indio's target?"

The hunter shrugged. "The same way you probably did, Colonel. I gathered every scrap of information I could on Indio. Then I tried fitting the scraps together every which way and the answer always came up the same—El Paso."

The Colonel nodded, uncorked the bottle and replenished their glasses. The hunter leaned his elbows on the table.

"After a year-and-a-half in prison he needs money—*big* money. Indio never did play penny ante. And he needs to pull off something really sensational to polish up the pride and reputation that got pretty badly tarnished when he let himself get caught. The answer *had* to be El Paso—the richest and toughest to crack bank in the territory."

"Good thinking, boy," the Colonel said. "Almost precisely the way I figured it out. But tell me, suppose you'd guessed wrong and his men hadn't showed up here as they did. What would you have figured to do then?"

The hunter grinned faintly. "Put a different bait on my hook and go on fishing. Maybe I'd get word to him about a little weakness or two in the bank's security system. I spotted a couple and I'm pretty sure you did, too."

"You're pretty sharp, lad," the Colonel said, lifting his glass in salute. "That's a good fourth reason for our teaming up. I'll tell you what I'll do. For reasons of my own, I'm going to kill Indio myself, and I won't let any man stand in my way. But I'll let you have the whole ten thousand on him and I'll settle for the smaller bounties on the rest of his men."

"Oh, no you don't," the hunter said. "That would be a pretty good deal, all right—for you. I happen to know the others will add up to more than the reward on Indio."

"How do you know that?"

"I have my source of information. For instance, there's four thousand on Nino, three on the Wild One, two on Blackie . . ."

"Correction," the Colonel said. "Blackie's only worth one." He opened a small black notebook and pointed to a name on a neatly penned list. "See? Altogether they add up to just ten thousand."

The other studied the list over the Colonel's shoulder. "There are some you haven't got down and they'll add up to quite a bit more. Still, I might just take you up on that partnership proposition."

They lifted their glasses. "To the partnership."

"With no tricks," the hunter warned.

"No tricks."

The hunter sat down, drawing his chair closer. "Now, then, the first thing we have to do is figure out some way to get them in the middle."

"Right. One to hit them from the outside and one from the inside. That's the only sure way. That means one of us is going to have to join up with Indio's gang."

"Yeah? And why are you looking straight at me when you say 'one of us'?"

"Because none of Indio's boys know you. But after that little byplay in the saloon, the Wild One would catch one look at me and his hump would burn."

"Yeah, and so would your tail. So I'm elected to the post of honour. Maybe you've got an idea how I should go about getting myself a nice warm welcome from a pack of wolves that would be suspicious of their own mothers? Do I just ride in and say, 'Howdy, friends. You don't know me but I'm a man you can trust. I've come to enlist in your gallant army'. Or do you think maybe it would help if I took Indio a bunch of roses?"

"Well-l-l," the Colonel said solemnly, "you could do that, but I have a better suggestion. Instead of roses, take him Sancho Perez."

"And who the hell is Sancho Perez?"

"A friend of Indio's and one of his most valuable hands. Indio's mighty unhappy because right now, when he needs him the most, Sancho's butt is planted for a four-year sit in the Alamagordo jail."

"How come you know all this?"

The Colonel smiled faintly. "I have my source of information, too, son."

"Alamagordo," the hunter mused, feeling for one of his *cigarros*. "I've seen that jug and it's no straw shack. We'll have to figure out a mighty good scheme to spring Sancho."

"This," said the Colonel, "is a fifty-fifty partnership. My contribution to the pot is the idea. The execution of it will have to be yours."

He got up and walked to the window. The other looked up at him, narrow eyed. "Tell me something, Colonel. Were you ever young?"

"Yes, boy, as young as you and every bit as reckless. And then, one day, something happened—something that suddenly made life very precious to me, and hanging on to it all important."

"What was that?" the hunter asked. When there

was no reply, he added, "Or is that question indiscreet?"

The Colonel turned slowly. "No, the question isn't indiscreet—but the answer could be."

The older man reached into a vest pocket and brought out a thick gold watch on a chain. The lid snapped open and the thin tinkle of chimes filled the room. The Colonel stood motionless, staring at a photograph inside the lid, lost in some dark memory.

After a time the hunter took his hat and went out, closing the door very softly behind him.

CHAPTER 10

MANY miles to the west, the same melody was tinkling from an identical watch, lying open on Indio's palm. The bandit sat slumped on a bench, eyes half-closed, withdrawn, lost in a dark memory of his own. As always, when the sound of the chimes awakened the haunting memory, he relived it all too sharply.

He had been walking along a dark street, close to the houses, when he heard the chimes for the first time. The sound was sifting thinly from a partly open window. Indio tiptoed closer and peered into a lighted bedroom. A girl, scarcely more than a child, sat cross-legged on the bed. She wore only a thin robe whose fabric did little to conceal the lush curves of her fresh, young body.

The watch lay open in front of her. She was listening to the elfin melody, her hands clasped, a look of childlike rapture on her lovely face. Lust for both the girl and the unique watch seized Indio and shook him, filling his veins with fire.

A young boy suddenly came into view. He sat down on the bed and put his arms around the girl, caressing her intimately and murmuring something about her favourite wedding present. At the sight, Indio's face twisted with savage rage. He snatched out his pistol and moved on cat feet to the front door.

The young lovers had forgotten to bar it.

The boy's caresses were growing more ardent and demanding. He leaned over suddenly and closed the watch, cutting off the chimes. He pulled the laughing girl against him and nuzzled her throat. After a moment her arms went around him and her young body snuggled closer to his.

The boy reached out to move the watch and saw the sinister figure standing in the doorway. For an instant he went rigid with shock. Then he yelled and flung himself off the bed toward the intruder. Indio's gun thundered, the heavy slugs literally hurling the slim youth back against the wall. The boy pitched forward, then lay unmoving, blood spurting from his shattered chest.

On the bed, the girl was paralysed with horror, her mouth straining open to a shriek that would not come. Indio strode to the bed and snatched up the watch. Then he stood looking down, feasting blazing eyes on the cowering girl. His rough hand shot out, tore the thin robe off her young body and hurled it aside. He took a moment longer to savour the prize. Then he was on her like an animal, growling, whimpering, slavering...

On the bench at the bandit headquarters, Indio sprang up with a strangled yell, his eyes wild. He beat at his head with clenched fists, pawed at his eyes, cupped palms over his ears—anything to cut off the flow of memory, to hold back the remainder of the horrible scene.

* * *

In the darkness, the prisoner, Sancho Perez, awoke suddenly with a feeling that something had touched his face. He felt his cheek cautiously, fearful of a scorpion or a venomous spider. He felt nothing. Then a pebble flying through the barred window fell on the cell floor.

Sancho sat up sharply, gaping at the silhouette of a man's head outside. A hand moved to the lips in a gesture of silence, then stabbed urgently toward Sancho's bunk. The bandit sat, open-mouthed and uncomprehending. The hand vanished, then reappeared, reaching through the bars to set a small cylindrical object against the iron frame.

Sancho still didn't understand. Then the hand took a lighted cigar from an invisible mouth and held it to the object. Sparks suddenly flew as a fuse sputtered to life. Sancho yelled, "Dynamite!" and dived for the farthest corner of his cell, dragging mattress and blankets over himself for a shield.

The night exploded in a blast of flame and fury, driving the breath from Sancho's lungs. But otherwise he was unharmed. He scrambled up, gasping, and saw a great gaping hole where the front of his cell had been. Down below, a stranger wearing a brown poncho sat on a saddled horse, holding the reins of another. The stranger gestured impatiently. Sancho hit the ground running and vaulted into the waiting saddle.

"Come on," the stranger barked. "You don't want to keep Indio waiting."

The great reunion, the Man With No Name, reflected sardonically, was poignantly touching. The bandits crowded Sancho, whooping and pounding his back. Indio shoved his way through and caught the arrival in a crushing bear hug.

"Sancho! Ah, my great and good friend, Sancho! And they told me you had been put away in the prison for four years—four long years without my Sancho."

"That is what *they* thought, too, Indio, but we fooled them, didn't we? Four years? Ho! Four little weeks only, and here I am, free and back with you, *amigo*."

Indio stepped back and for the first time became aware of the tall stranger in the brown poncho. The Mexican's hand whipped to his side, the fingers flexed for an instant draw. He scowled at the impassive man before him.

"Sancho! This man who came with you. Who is he?"

"My great and good friend, Indio—he's the man who blew up the jail and set me free."

"Why Sancho? Why should he do all that for you? Did you ask him why?"

Sancho gaped at his chief. "But—but I thought you sent him to get me out, Indio."

"I sent no one. I never saw this man before in my life." Indio stepped forward, his hand close to his gun, his face taut with suspicion. The others faded back, leaving the two to face one another. Indio rasped, "Talk and talk straight, you! Who are you and why did you do this thing for Sancho? Why should you take so much risk and trouble for one you do not even know? Answer me."

The Man With No Name took his time getting out a stubby *cigarro* and making sure it was properly lit. He dropped the match to the floor. Indio gestured impatiently. "The answer—and the truth!"

"If you insist, Indio," the stranger said. "The truth is, there's such a fat bounty posted on all your heads that I simply couldn't resist making a try for it. I decided the best way to collect would be to get in good with you, tag along on your next big raid and watch for a chance to turn you in to the law."

He puffed on his *cigarro,* smiling calmly and pleasantly around the circle of stunned faces. Nino was the first to break the stunned silence. His hand flashed to his hip and his gun blasted deafeningly in the closed room. The end of the bounty hunter's *cigarro* vanished in flying shreds and sparks.

Without the slightest show of emotion, the Man With No Name examined the remaining stub with mild interest, then put it back in his mouth. He walked toward Nino, holding out his hand.

"You put out my light, friend. I'm afraid I'll have to trouble you for a match."

Like a man hypnotised, the bandit got a match from his vest pocket and handed it over. The hunter calmly relit the stump with a hand as steady as a rock.

Indio suddenly gave a bark of laughter. "Enough. That, my friend, was the one answer that would make me believe you are all right, a man to be trusted.

Now that you are one of us, by what name do we call you, *amigo*?"

The hunter eyed the bandit steadily, puffing his *cigarro* in pointed silence. After a moment, Indio shrugged. "No matter. What is a name, anyhow? A handle. And you, my friend, do not strike me as a man to be pushed around by a handle."

The others were relaxing visibly, hands dropping away from their guns, hostility fading from their hard faces. At Indio's gesture they dropped down on chairs or benches, forming a rough semicircle around their chief's seat. Nino, still looking dazed, made room for the hunter on a bench.

"Man With No Name," Indio said, grinning, "if it is the reward that brings you here, you have arrived at exactly the right moment. For, after tomorrow, my friend, those rewards will go up and up, clear to the sky. Even I will be tempted by them." He grinned wolfishly. "Tomorrow, *amigo,* we do the impossible, we rob the mighty Bank Of El Paso of a million dollars. You are just in time to fill an important place in my plans."

He leaned forward, eyes glittering. "A few miles from El Paso is a little town called Santa Cruz. The first thing tomorrow morning, four men will hold up the bank there, shooting and killing every person in sight. Those four will be Blackie, Chico, Paco . . . and *you, Senor* No Name. When you flee, you will leave a clear trail that will draw every gun after you. They will telegraph for the posse from El Paso and we will take care of the few left behind."

"Clever," the hunter said. "Then what?"

"At the right time, you will shake them off your trail and join us at Las Palmeras. Then we will all ride to a place I have selected and there, my friend, we will divide up a million dollars."

The hunter got to his feet, picked up the saddle and blankets he had left inside the door and headed for the stairs.

"Where do you think you are going?" Indio barked.

The hunter paused. "Why, if there's going to be a lot of shooting tomorrow, I have to get my rest." He smiled at the band and tramped off up the stairs.

CHAPTER 11

THE four rode out in the waning hours of the night. Dawn found them looking down from the shoulder of a mountain on to the sleeping town of Santa Cruz. With several hours to kill before the bank would open, they found a hidden place among the rocks, built a small fire and brewed coffee. Afterward, they rolled up in their blankets.

The others were soon snoring but the hunter lay, wide awake, staring up into the brightening sky. When it was full daylight he threw off his blanket, got a tin cup from his saddle and poured himself a cup of coffee, kept hot on the dying embers. He was sipping the bitter brew when Blackie awoke and sat up. The bandit grinned at the tall man.

"Hey, *amigo*—you know, when you told that crazy story last night, about being a bounty hunter, I really fell for it for a while. Some big joke, eh, *amigo*?"

The hunter eyed him steadily. "Who said I was joking?"

The outlaw blinked, his jaw going slack. Then comprehension knifed through the daze. He cried thickly, "By God, then it's true," and snatched at his gun.

The tin cup clattered on the rocks. The noise, and Blackie's yell, awoke the others. They were scrambling up, reaching for their own weapons, when the hunter's gun blasted. The heel of his left hand fanned the hammer so swiftly that the three shots sounded almost as one, the echoes racketing against the mountain.

The Man With No Name reloaded and holstered his pistol before dragging the three bodies to a concealing niche between the rocks. He stood for a moment, looking down at them, his lips moving as he calculated the bounty they would bring. Then, after turning the other mounts loose, he swung into his saddle and rode leisurely down to Santa Cruz.

A small shanty beside the railroad tracks served as a combination depot, telegraph office and living quarters for the agent. He was a very old man, thin and dried up.

When the hunter stepped noiselessly inside, the old man was bent over a small stove, breaking breakfast eggs into a sizzling pan. He was unaware of the other's presence until a hand came in to pluck the last egg from his fingers and crack it against the rim of the frying pan. The agent squeaked in alarm and jumped back, staring at the tall man in the brown poncho.

"Wh-what do you want, m-mister?"

"Indio and his gang just robbed your bank, Pop, and rode out, leaving a clear trail. They killed several people. I'll tend your eggs while you sit down at that telegraph and flash the alarm to El Paso and the other towns close by. Tell 'em to send every available man to run down the gang."

"Now, you lookee here, mister. I don't know what

your dad-blasted game is, but you're lyin' through your teeth. The bank's right over there and my hearin's plenty good. I didn't hear no shots and I sure would have knowed if there was any funny goin's-on like you tell about there."

The hunter twitched the end of the poncho aside and laid his hand on his gun. "Pop, you're liable to hear a shot right here in this room if you don't skedaddle over to that instrument and do what I told you."

The old man gulped, sidled warily past the intruder and slid into the operator's chair. He flicked switches and began to work the telegraph key. The hunter stood close behind him, reading the broken clatter from the sounder, nodding approvingly. He turned away once to test the eggs with a fork and found them not yet cooked.

As the last clatter of the message died away, the hunter reached over and yanked the sender from its base, ripping out the wires. He swung the chair around, tied the old man's hands loosely behind the chair's back and gagged him with a dish towel. In the doorway he paused and nodded toward the stove.

"Don't let the eggs burn, Pop."

He mounted and raced out at a dead run, following the railroad tracks toward El Paso. A short way out he saw a broad trail where a large band of mounted men had crossed the tracks. Someone with a steady hand had shot both insulators off the telegraph pole, severing the wires and cutting El Paso off from all communication to the north.

Moments later, the hunter heard the thunder of hoofbeats from the trail ahead. He turned his horse into a concealing niche between rocks and watched a large and heavily armed sheriff's posse pound past, heading in the direction of Santa Cruz. He nodded with satisfaction. So far, every detail of Indio's clever plan was working perfectly.

The main street of El Paso was deserted and empty when The Man With No Name rode in and swung down at the hotel hitchrail. Colonel Mortimer sat at his window, smoking his pipe. He looked down and made a small gesture to indicate that nothing had occurred as yet. The tall man gave a slight nod of understanding and stepped into the space between the hotel and the adjoining building, where a wooden outside stairway offered partial concealment but gave him a clear view of the bank.

The waiting and the watching dragged on. At closing time the director of the bank locked the door behind the inside guard and walked away. The outside patrols separated to begin their tramping rounds.

The two watchers exchanged baffled looks. They had expected the bandits to strike while the bank was open, depending on the size of their force and their deadly guns to handle any feeble opposition. What could they do now, with the bank locked and guarded, inside and out, and supposedly invulnerable?

The Colonel leaned out to look down the street and then jerked his head back inside. He gestured violently. The hunter peered cautiously around the corner of the building and stiffened. Indio and his entire gang were riding up the road in a tight bunch, followed by a heavy, canvas-topped freight wagon.

At the edge of town they paused to study the empty street for signs of an ambush. At last, Indio gestured and they separated into two groups that swung right and left to circle the narrow buildings from two sides. The covered wagon followed the group that was to pass behind the bank.

The hunter looked up at the Colonel and scratched his head. The Colonel nodded with equal perplexity, unable to fathom the baffling manœuvre. His narrowed gaze followed the pairs of guards circling the bank. One pair was marching before the bank's door, then it vanished around the rear corner. Moments later the second pair appeared, stepping towards the front. For the minutes it would take them to go around and meet again, the rear of the bank would be unwatched and unprotected.

The second patrol was halfway to the front when it happened. There was a thunderous blast that rocked the ground and shook the buildings. A huge column of dust and debris lifted skyward above the rear of the bank. The guards whirled and ran towards the explosion, cocking their rifles.

Upstairs, Colonel Mortimer spun away from the window, the long pistol in his hand. The hunter snatched his own weapon and then froze as part of Indio's gang streamed in to gun down the running guards. As the bandits pounded from view around the bank corner, the Man With No Name darted across the street and through a narrow alley between buildings to a spot where he could see without being seen by the outlaws.

So perfectly timed and rehearsed was the entire action that he almost missed what was happening at the bank. The covered wagon was backed up below a great, gaping hole that had been blown completely through the rear wall into the vault room. Four bandits with ropes tied to their saddle horns were pulling at the camouflaged safe, dragging it out on to a ramp of heavy timbers that slanted down into the back of the wagon.

The heavy safe teetered, then slid down under the canvas top. As it thudded against the wagon bed, a whip cracked and the team lunged into their harnesses. They wheeled and set off at a gallop, following the bandit pack already racing out of town.

People were streaming towards the wreckage. The hunter looked vainly around for the tall figure of the Colonel, then ran to join the curious throng. The body of the inside guard sprawled in death at the edge of the hole.

The hunter scowled, trying to figure out how Indio's men could have planted so much dynamite in so brief a time. There had been no sounds of chopping or digging in the interval. Then he saw that amid the debris on the ground were chunks of adobe covered with a dark substance. He touched it and found it to be pitch, still warm and sticky. The answer came to him then.

They had coated a bundle of dynamite sticks with the pitch, lighted the fuse and flung it against the wall.

It had stuck there in precisely the right place to open the wall directly behind the cash-laden safe.

He whirled and ran back to his horse. Vaulting into the saddle he raced off at a dead run in the wake of the vanished bandits. His slitted eyes were like burning coals in the taut mask of his face.

The broad trail turned in the direction of the agreed meeting place and entered a winding pass. The Man With No Name burst out of the far end and gave the reins a sudden jerk that set the bay back on its haunches. It skidded to a stop with its nose almost against the lathered flank of the black horse that blocked the trail.

"Going somewhere, *partner*?" asked Colonel Douglas Mortimer softly. The tawny eyes were narrow. "You wouldn't, by any remote chance, be running out on the job just because our first plan didn't work out quite the way we expected?"

"No, I'm not running out on the job," the other said savagely. "I'm going after Indio and his pack of killers—and I'm going *alone*. As of right now, our little partnership is dissolved."

"Now, now, boy. Let's wait until we've cooled off and then talk this all over, quietly and sensibly."

"Bull sweat! All we've done is talk and we haven't seen one cent of cash to show for it. I've been reasonable and I've waited to do things your way. Well, I'm through waiting so get the hell out of my way."

"Cool down, boy. Cool down a moment. Look, Indio was simply too cagey to let you in on more than the first part of his great scheme. It couldn't be helped because we couldn't anticipate that."

"Why couldn't we anticipate it? You were the great brain, the one who had their strategy all mapped out. How come you didn't have *that* part mapped, genius?" The hunter gathered up the reins. "It doesn't matter, anyhow. I'm going to get Indio."

The Colonel sighed. "All right, but in the mood you're in now, you're more likely to get yourself killed. I'd better ride along to cover your back and take a hand if you need me."

"Look," the hunter said through gritted teeth, "I'm the one who has the date with Indio—just me, personally. And I'm not letting anybody get in the way of my keeping it—*alone*."

He kicked the bay's flanks and crowded past.

"All right, my boy," the Colonel said. He sighed. "I'm sorry to have to do this but . . ." He whipped out the long-barrelled pistol and fired point-blank at the other's back.

A searing pain flashed along the side of the hunter's neck, followed by a gush of warm blood. He put his hand to the shallow wound and twisted to glare at the Colonel, who was calmly replacing the spent shell. "Why, you . . ."

"Uh, uh, uh," the older man interrupted wagging a finger. "Easy, boy. You don't seem to realise that I just saved your life."

"What the hell do you mean by that?"

"Think a moment. I'm guessing you sent that call for help from Santa Cruz. It would fit my idea that Indio meant to create some such diversion. If Indio sent you, then he must have sent at least three others he knew he could trust, along with you. Now, if you planned to ride back, without a mark or a scratch, and make him swallow a cock-and-bull story of the others being gunned by the law, you're a bigger fool than you seem to expect Indio to be. *Now* you've got some proof that just might convince him."

The hunter brought down his bloodied hand, wiped it on a handkerchief, then tucked the kerchief into the neck of the poncho against the shallow wound.

"Thanks," he said, at last. "It was kind of a dumb thing, at that."

"Hmmm! Do I detect the faintest hint that the partnership might just possibly be glued back together again?"

"Oh, hell, I suppose so."

The Colonel smiled. "That's splendid, because the stakes have just gone up by forty thousand, my boy. That's the amount the bank was offering for the return of its money as I rode out at your heels."

"More talk," the other said, but he grinned as he said it.

"Now, here's what you'll have to try to do. It will take Indio a long, long time to crack that safe so he'll have a spot in mind where he can open it at his leisure. Your job is to convince him that whatever spot he's picked is bad. Convince him his best move is to head north, up the river, to a perfect hideout you know. The best way to get the whole gang is by ambush, and the best spot for an ambush is up the canyon to the north. You get him to go that way and I'll be waiting to open the festivities. Make sense, boy?"

He held out his hand and after a long moment, the other took it. "Makes sense—partner."

The Man With No Name was nearing Indio's camp when he heard the gunfire. It sounded like a pitched battle between large forces. Then he topped a rock ridge and saw that Indio's whole gang was lined up, blazing away at the wooden cabinet that disguised the stolen safe. As he drew near, a burly outlaw strode over and wrenched away the riddled wood, exposing the heavy iron.

The bandits whirled at the sound of the bay's hoofs, their hands streaking to their guns, then hovering there as they eyed the hunter with deep suspicion. Indio straightened from inspecting the safe.

"You! What happened to the others? Dead?"

The hunter nodded and slid down wearily. The handkerchief at his neck was a sodden wad and dried blood had spread a dark stain down the poncho. The Man With No Name clung to the saddle for support.

"That damn telegram," he said thickly. "We were clear and heading for El Paso when we ran straight into a posse from some town close by. The boys never had a chance."

The bandit Groggy took two steps and grabbed the front of the brown poncho. "And you left good men to die while you saved your own skin, you yellow bast . . ."

The knife edge of an open palm flashed up to knock away the clawing hand. A granite fist smashed Groggy full in the face. The bandit flew backward, rolling in the dust, clawing at his gun. Indio took a quick step and kicked, sending the weapon flying.

The outlaw chief picked up a rifle, strode to the hunter and used the muzzle to poke away the stiffening handkerchief. He studied the wound intently, then nodded.

"Powder burns. He wasn't running away when he took that one. He took his part." He turned to the others. "All right, get moving and get that safe loaded again. We're heading for a safe place where we can get it open."

"Which way, Indio?" the hunter asked.

"North, up the river into the broken country." He peered narrowly at the tall man's face. "Why? You got any better ideas?"

"If I wanted to lay an ambush, I couldn't think of a better place than those narrow canyons upriver, Indio. I'd say our best bet is a quick dash south, over the border, where they can't chase you for fear of running into a troop of *Rurales*."

"Mmm!" The bandit fingered his chin thoughtfully, paced a few steps and wheeled around. "You're right about the north and you could be right about the south. But me, I like to make my own plans. So we'll go east to a little place I know—Agua Caliente. It's a town where nobody asks questions and nobody tells tales."

The tall man fought to suppress a grin of delight. It was better than he had dared hope. The Colonel would be thrown completely off the track, leaving him free to deal with Indio in his own good time and on his own terms. And keep every penny of the huge bounty for himself.

They came over a range of low hills and looked down on a cluster of connected adobe shacks lining a narrow street. Indio lifted his hand and they reined in. He looked at the man in the poncho, his eyes sharp.

"There, my friend, is Agua Caliente. It looks dead, does it not? Like a morgue, perhaps. And it could so easily become one if a man is not careful. They don't like strangers one bit down there, do they, Groggy?"

"Hell, they don't like *anybody* down there, Indio."

The bandit leader twisted in his saddle and jerked a thumb toward the hunter. "I was just thinking—have any of you ever seen our new friend, here, handle a gun? Do any of us know if he is fast or slow, if he has guts or worms in his belly?"

The bandits shook their heads and turned hostile, suspicious glares on the tall man. The Wild One fondled his gun, licking his lips. Indio chuckled.

"It is time we found out exactly how dependable he would be to us if we found ourselves in bad trouble. Now, fortunately, we have here a simple way to find these things out. We will let our friend ride into Agua Caliente ahead of us, alone, to let them know we are approaching."

There was a cackle of appreciative laughter. The hunter shrugged indifferently, lifted a hand in casual salute and rode away down the winding trail. He reached under the poncho and got out a *cigarro* and a match.

As he neared the town a woman darted from a

shack, snatched up two small children playing in the street and ducked back inside. The slam of closing shutters and the thud of door bars ran ahead of the hunter along the rows of houses. Down the street a heavily armed man stepped into view from behind a wall, followed by two more. They watched his approach in hostile silence.

He swung out of the saddle, hitched the bay and started a slow walk toward the trio, throwing the end of the poncho over his shoulder to clear the gun at his hip. A whacking noise drew his attention to the side. Behind one of the houses, a small boy was jumping up and down, swinging a long stick in a vain effort to knock off an orange from a cluster just out of reach.

The hunter's draw was lightning fast. He fired from the hip, without sighting, and the orange fell to the ground. The boy gaped at him, then snatched up the fruit. The Man With No Name shot again and another fell.

Behind and above him another gun slammed twice and two more oranges dropped from the tree. He whirled, staring up at the frock-coated figure of Colonel Mortimer, standing on a small balcony.

"Nice shooting," the hunter said sourly.

"Thank you, my boy."

The Colonel reloaded and holstered the long pistol. He vaulted the balcony railing and landed lightly in the street. He nodded toward a door at the side. "I was about to sit down to a miserable repast when you arrived. Care to join me? The only thing this *taberna* —this tavern—can boast is that it is the only one in town."

As they tramped into the dingy bar, the hunter growled, "Do you mind telling me just how in hell you happened to turn up here, of all places."

"A matter of simple reasoning, lad. Knowing your eagerness to get Indio on your own, I told you to steer him north, knowing full well you'd do the exact opposite and urge him to head south. But, knowing Indio's suspicious nature, I was sure he'd do neither. Westward, the country is too populous for him. That left the east, and the most likely spot east was here."

The Colonel sat down at a small table and attacked a bowl of beans. The tall man ordered a rum and leaned on the bar, sipping it and glaring disgustedly at the dirty wall.

The door slammed open and Indio tramped in with his band, roaring. "Tequil afor all of us." He slapped the hunter's back. "We heard shots. Did you run into trouble?"

"Nothing I couldn't handle."

The hunchback was lifting his drink when he discovered the figure at the table. The glass clattered to the bar. He cat-footed to the table, the muscle jumping in his cheek, a crazy light in the pale eyes. He bent over the table.

"The smoker. The match-scratcher. Remember me, *amigo*?"

The Colonel glanced up indifferently, shook his head and resumed his eating. "Can't say that I do, friend."

"You remember me, all right," the Wild One spat.

"El Paso—the hotel saloon."

The Colonel examined the twitching face with mild interest. "Well, well. It's a small world, isn't it?"

"And a bad one," the hunchback squalled, shaking with the intensity of his rage. "Very, very bad for some people. Now, come on and light another match. Here is my shoulder. Light up the way you did before."

The Colonel took another bite. "Sorry, my boy. I only strike a match when I'm ready to smoke, and I don't smoke until I have finished my meal. Perhaps, if you care to come back in ten minutes . . ."

"Now!" the hunchback screamed. "Right now! In ten minutes you'll be sizzling in hell. Get on your feet! Cucillo, count to three."

Indio and the others were watching in avid fascination. The bandit Cucillo began the count. "One!"

The Colonel broke off a morsel of hard bread and chewed it with relish.

"Two!"

He dipped up a spoonful of beans.

"Three!"

The Wild One's clawed hand slapped down on his gun. The Colonel moved his arm and a small derringer dropped from his sleeve into his palm. It cracked and the hunchback's face went slack. He fell against the table and dragged it over with his fall.

The long pistol was suddenly in the Colonel's hand, moving to cover the group by the bar. Indio gestured impatiently.

"Stop it, all of you. And put away that cannon so we can talk. Just who are you?"

"The man who can open that safe for you."

Indio's eyes narrowed. "What safe, *senor*?"

"The one you took from the Bank of El Paso. It was my bad luck that you got there a little ahead of me, but I tagged along on the chance that I might salvage a little something for my time and trouble."

"So . . . ?"

"So, if you open the safe your way, with dynamite, you'll destroy half the bank notes in the blast. I'm the only man in the territory who knows how to get it open without harming a single bill."

"For how much?"

"Five thousand."

"Too much. Two thousand is my limit."

The Colonel shrugged indifferently. "Five is my price. Take it or leave it."

After a moment Indio jerked his head toward the door. "Come along, then, and earn it."

The Colonel unsnapped the valise at his feet and got out a small twist drill, a medicine dropper and a bottle of yellowish fluid. He followed the bandit leader out into the street.

The gang had taken up quarters in an abandoned *hacienda* by the row of shacks. The safe stood in the small courtyard. At the Colonel's order they tipped it on to its back, with the lock and handle on top. He stripped off the frock coat, put a knee on the safe and began to drill a circle of small holes all around the massive lock.

When he had finished, he opened the bottle and used the dropper to fill each hole with the yellow fluid.

The sharp stench of acid rose. There was a frying sound and then smoke rose from the holes as the powerful fluid ate into the iron. After a time, the sizzling died away and the smoke faded. The Colonel tugged at the handle and the safe door came open.

The bandits crowded in, yelling, reaching for the stacks of banknotes and bags of gold pieces. Indio's voice rang out above the uproar.

"Get your hands out of there and get back, all of you. Now listen to me. To steal so much was easy, but to keep it will be a different matter. Every man in the territory is out hunting us now. All they have to do is catch one of us with some of this money on him and we will all be dead men. Nino, bring the chest."

Nino and a companion vanished into the stable and came out carrying a heavy chest with a massive lock. They opened it and began transferring the money from the safe into it.

"What we're going to do," Indio continued, "is wait an entire month, if necessary. When I decide the hunt has cooled down enough, we will divide the money and each man will get his full share." He looked at the Colonel, "You, my friend, will also wait the month to get your money."

The Colonel shrugged. "The grub in that tavern stinks, but with no choice, I suppose I can stand it for a month." He took his coat and equipment and walked off without a glance at the man in the brown poncho.

When the safe was empty, Indio locked the chest with a key he wore on a thong around his neck. He and Nino carried the case into an inner room of the stable and came out, locking the heavy door behind them. The hunter watched the entire activity with glittering eyes, then turned and strolled with elaborate casualness toward the tavern.

Indio and his lieutenant took the bedrooms, the Colonel stayed at the tavern and the rest bedded down on the floor of a storeroom. It was midnight before the hunter was certain the bandits were deep in sleep. He got up soundlessly, stepped over the sleeping figures and slipped out into the night.

He came up silently behind the low-roofed building that held Indio's makeshift strongroom, half-expecting to find either the bandit chief or Nino on guard. He waited for some time, crouching in the deep shadows, until he was sure no pacing figure would appear. Then he sprang up, caught the edge of the roof and swung himself on to the loosely fitting tiles that covered it.

It took him only moments to lift the tiles aside until he had an opening big enough to let him wriggle through between the rafters, hung by his hands a moment, then dropped to the earthen floor.

From somewhere close by came the scrape of a match and light sprung up from the wick of a stubby candle. Colonel Mortimer said softly, "It took you long enough to get here."

The soldier put away his long pistol as the other holstered the weapon he had snatched.

"Have any trouble with the lock, Colonel?"

"My dear fellow, as you must know by now, I'm not exactly an amateur in dealing with locks. Afterward,

Indio's chest had such a pitifully empty appearance that I left the reward poster with his picture on it in place of the bank notes." The Colonel picked up a pair of bulging saddlebags from behind a box. "It's all here—a million dollars. Take it and get going. I'll meet you by our horses as soon as I've fixed this lock so nobody can tell it's been tampered with."

"You know," the other said, "I almost wish I could be here to watch Indio's face when he discovers the money is gone and tries to figure how it could have leaked out of a locked chest when he's the only man alive who has the key."

"You're liable to be here, watching it all," the Colonel said grimly, "if you don't get a move on and get out of here."

The old soldier knelt in front of the chest and gave the heavy padlock a final tug to make sure it was securely latched. Then, using a dab of putty kneaded with lamp black and iron filings, he completely obliterated the marks of his drill.

Meanwhile, the hunter had stepped up on a box and vanished through the opening in the roof. He slid down to the edge, pulling the bulging saddlebags behind him. When a quick look down showed no visible danger, he flopped over on his belly, legs hanging over the edge, and eased himself cautiously down.

One foot landed squarely on a human shoulder and a hard hand closed on his ankle.

His action, then, was sheer reflex. His arm snapped straight and the saddlebags went sailing up over the peak of the roof and out of sight. He heard the faint rustle as they landed in a tree on the far side and hoped the man below was too preoccupied to notice. Then he dropped to the ground.

The hard, cold muzzle of a pistol rammed into his middle. Indio grinned at him, reaching under the brown poncho to snatch away his own gun. *"Senor, senor,"* the bandit said softly, shaking his head, "you make *so* much trouble for people with your foolish, wandering ways."

There was a soft scraping sound overhead and the polished boots of Colonel Douglas Mortimer appeared. With elaborate mock courtesy, Indio put his free hand under one and eased the tall man to the ground. He snatched the long pistol from under the frock coat and stepped back.

"Will you precede me to the courtyard, *senors*? We are about to enjoy a small *fiesta* in honour of our great triumph—and you two are to be the guests of honour."

CHAPTER 12

INDIO'S shout brought the rest of the gang tumbling out, eyes still heavy with sleep. They gaped at the two captives.

"My friends," Indio said. "Allow me to introduce two professional bounty killers whose luck has just run out. Guard them carefully but do not harm them while I learn what mischief they might have done. Nino, come with me."

Almost running, Indio led the way to the strong-room. While he unlocked the heavy timbered door, Nino lit a candle. Through the open door the captives could see the bandit chief kneel at the chest to tug at the padlock. Satisfied, he relocked the door and came back, a look of sharp relief on his swarthy face.

"All is well." He faced the pair, eyes glittering. "It is too bad all your trouble was for nothing. You could not get into the money chest without using a crowbar to break off the lock or an axe to chop into the chest. Either would have made a great noise and brought us all running.'

He grinned at his gang, savouring his moment of triumph to its fullest. "*Amigos,* you see before you two wicked, wicked men who do evil things. They hunt down and kill other men for money. They sneak about in the dark of night, seeking to steal what is not theirs.

Such bad deeds should not go unpunished, and I leave it to you to see that they are not. Teach these two a lesson, *amigos,* but do not kill them." He paused, then added softly, "Not just yet."

From the corner of his mouth, the hunter murmured, "Well, come on, genius. Don't you have some bright ideas for getting us out of this?"

"No ideas," the Colonel said sadly. "Only wishes that I very much fear are not going to be fulfilled."

They tried to put up a good fight but the odds against them made it hopeless. They got in a few solid punches and then they were simply overwhelmed by numbers, their own blows smothered by the crush of hard bodies and the hail of slamming fists. When they went down, they were stomped and kicked by savage boots. Again and again they struggled back to their feet, only to be knocked, reeling and dazed, from one eager bandit to another.

The hunter had the small satisfaction of putting two of his attackers out of action. Once he found space to swing and smashed a full-arm punch squarely into the face of the man known as Hughie. The hunter felt bone and cartilage splinter under his knuckles. The bandit flew backward, slammed into the watching Indio and both went rolling. Indio scrambled up, cursing, but the other lay unmoving for the remainder of the struggle.

A minute later, the hunter was sent sprawling to the ground, his arms outflung. The one called Groggy lifted a boot to mash the gun-hand to useless pulp. With his last reserve of strength, the hunter rolled over, caught the lifted foot with both hand and twisted viciously.

Groggy went into the air in a twisting somersault, yelling wildly. He came down on his back, his neck and shoulders hitting the ground with a jarring crash that left him out of breath and out of the fight. Beyond him, two bandits were pinning the Colonel's arms while a third slugged him in the belly. The Colonel's boot drove up and caught his chief tormentor full in the groin. The bandit screamed, high pitched like a woman, doubled over and stumbled away, feet spraddled wide apart.

Indio ended the carnage at last with a shot fired into the air. The men turned toward him, panting and exhausted. The Mexican chief stepped up and studied the two battered and bloody figures sprawled in the dust.

"Enough," he said. "Nino, see that they are securely tied and set a guard to watch them every moment. I want no tricks."

Groggy was struggling to his feet, still gasping for breath, his face dark with rage. "I can save you all that trouble with two bullets. Let me kill them both right here and have it over with."

"All things at their proper time, *amigo,*" Indio said. He studied the bandit thoughtfully. "You are a very lucky man, Groggy. You are all lucky men to have Indio do your thinking for you. Suppose these two were to be discovered near El Paso, each with his gun drawn and each killed by a shot from the other's weapon. If the good sheriff of El Paso were to find them so, and if he were to discover some of the bank's money on their persons, what do you suppose he might think, eh?"

The outlaw chief looked at his men, watching their faces light up with comprehension and break into admiring grins. He pointed. "Slim, you will take the first turn standing guard. Nino, you come with me. The rest of you get to sleep. Tomorrow there will be much work for all of us to do."

The two dishevelled figures, no more than half-conscious, were dragged into a storeroom. Their ankles were tightly lashed and their wrists bound together behind their backs. Leaving them far enough apart so neither could surreptitiously work on the other's ropes, the guard, Slim, built up the fire in the mud fireplace to hold back the night chill. He drew his *serape* closer around him and sat down with his back to the wall where he could keep both prisoners in full view.

In the little bedroom, Nino stared at his chief, his mouth sagging open, his face gone slack, his eyes wide with stunned incredulity. He backed up until his legs met the edge of the bed and then he sank down, shaking his head in slow disbelief.

"Indio," he managed at last, his voice no more than a croak. "Indio, are you positive these—these *things* you tell me I must do are your true wishes?"

"Amigo," the bandit leader said softly, "have you ever known Indio when he was not positive of what to do? I have never been more positive than I am tonight. There is no need for you to try to understand.

Just do everything exactly the way I have explained to you. Later, it will all become clear to you and you will see that it was the right thing to do. It is for us—for you and me, old friend. Now put it out of your mind and get some sleep. I will awaken you when it is the proper time."

After his lieutenant had gone, Indio took out the thick gold watch and snapped open the case. He dropped his face into his hands and sat, slumped and inert, listening to the magic of the tinkling chimes.

The night was still ink-dark but somewhere in the town a cock crowed his challenge to the coming dawn. The sound brought Indio to his feet. He went across the hall and stirred the sleeping figure of his lieutenant with the toe of his boot. Nino's eyes flew open and he sat up. "Now?"

"Now, *amigo*."

Nino got to his feet slowly, his eyes still puzzled. "Indio, you are still sure of this? Your mind has not changed?"

"My mind has not changed, Nino. Go quickly, now, and get it over with. There is no time to waste."

The other turned and went out slowly, still shaking his head. At the door of the storeroom, he stopped, looking in at the huddle of sleeping men. Most of them had blankets or *serapes* rolled tightly around them. Close to the warmth of the fire, the bandit Cucillo was snoring with his back to the wall, his head sagging, his mouth open. His *serape* had fallen open, exposing the hilt of the hunting knife tucked into his belt.

Nino went across on silent feet, looked carefully

around at the others, then gently pulled out the knife. Cucillo stirred momentarily but did not awaken. Nino held the knife closer to the fire and saw that the bandit's initials were crudely carved on the bone. He nodded with satisfaction and slipped out.

In the other storeroom the bandit Slim shivered and got to his feet. He bent over the prisoners, making sure they were asleep and still tightly secured, then went to put more wood on the fire. As he straightened up, a soft hiss made him whirl; his hand streaked to his gun, then dropped away.

Nino was in the doorway, beckoning urgently. "There has been a change in plans, Slim. Come outside, where those two cannot overhear, in case they are only pretending to be asleep, and I will explain. There is a matter Indio desires you to take care of for him at once."

"That suits me, Nino," Slim said. "I was gettin' just about fed up, anyhow, just sittin' here, starin' at them two."

He went out the door and across the courtyard at Nino's heels. The moment Slim disappeared, the pulped and purplish flesh around Colonel Mortimer's eyes stirred painfully and parted to reveal two glittering slits. He turned his head toward the figure in the brown poncho and saw a similar glint peep from the puffy bruises. The figure moved as if to roll toward him but the Colonel shook his head warningly, suppressing a groan at the movement.

"There wouldn't be time enough now," the older man whispered. "Besides, we'd better wait to find out what new scheme that devil has cooked up before we try to make a play."

"You're one damned hard man to put down for keeps, aren't you?"

The Colonel's mashed lips stirred in a grotesque travesty of a smile. "You didn't turn out to be such a snivelling quitter yourself when the chips were down—partner."

Outside, Nino stopped beside the *hacienda* wall and beckoned again. "Bend your head close, Slim. What I am about to tell you is for your ears alone, *amigo.*"

"Whisper it," Slim said. "I got good hearing."

He leaned forward. Nino put his left arm around the skinny shoulders and drew the other's ear close to his lips. He whispered softly, "What Indio wishes you to do for him, *amigo,* is . . ." His right hand set the point of the stolen knife just under Slim's rib cage and drove it upward to the hilt.

Nino's big hand shot up to muffle the death-yell. When the last aimless twitching of reflex stopped, he hoisted the scrawny figure to his shoulder and deposited it in the deep shadows, leaving the knife hilt jutting from the widening stain.

Nino drew his own knife, then, and went back to the room in which the two prisoners lay. He looked down at the motionless men and whispered softly. "Do not bother pretending you are both asleep, *amigos.* There is no time for games. In a few minutes the daylight will begin."

Bending, he sliced the thong binding the Colonel's

ankles, then freed his wrists. He pulled the man to his feet and held him until he could stand by himself. He drew the Colonel's long pistol from his own waistband and tucked it into the empty holster.

"I am sorry there are no bullets for your gun, my friend, but that is a matter you will attend to quickly, I am sure."

Nino bent over the other man and slashed away the bonds, then helped the hunter to his feet. He tucked the hunter's pistol into its holster. "It, too, is empty, *senor*. A thousand regrets."

The Colonel found a travesty of a voice and croaked, "What in the name of . . . ?"

Nino whirled around, finger to lips. "There is no time for questions and explanations. You must get out of here at once and get yourselves far away—so far that Indio cannot lay eyes or sights on you. Be quiet and *vamos!*"

The Colonel looked at his partner, standing rigid with disbelief. "What are we waiting for? *Vamonos*—let's go!"

They lurched past Nino and out into the dawn, hanging on to one another for support until circulation returned to their bound limbs and their battered muscles could be driven back to normal function. Nino stood in the doorway, shaking his head and watching the two vanish into the fading night.

Across the courtyard a match flamed in the deep shadows and Indio got to his feet, lighting a freshly rolled cigarette.

"It was perfect, Nino. You made every move exactly the way I told you. Now let us get on with the most important business of all, old friend."

CHAPTER 13

THE first pale colour was spreading across the eastern sky and the shadows that hid the land were becoming more grey than black. The two men stumbled on, still clinging together, every move a shrieking agony of resentful muscles.

"I've got just one small question," the hunter panted at last. "Do you, by any slim chance, have an idea where we're going to hole up in the condition we're in? We've got no ammunition for our guns, no strength in our arms or legs and, if you ask me for a straight answer, no goddam sense or excuse for still being alive."

"Why," the Colonel said in a tone of mild surprise, "we're going precisely where Nino and Indio intended us to go, of course. We have no choice, really."

"You mean to tell me you've got the faintest idea what all these crazy doings are about?"

"Why, of course, my boy. It's utterly simple, really, and fiendishly clever, as well. You'd have it all figured out in a moment if your wits hadn't been all scrambled out of shape by that fearful beating you took. Just hang on for a few more steps, my boy, and we'll be able to rest while we plan out our next move. This time there will be no painful slip-ups in completing our agreed enterprise."

"You mean you still aren't ready to give up and admit our string might just be all played out?"

The Colonel touched the hard lump of the gold watch in his vest pocket, somehow miraculously overlooked by their captors. "As long as Indio's feet tramp the earth and his lungs draw a breath, my string will never be played out."

The pale white cubes of Agua Caliente's adobes loomed out of the fading darkness. They had circled around and were now back where they had started. They stumbled down the single street until the Colonel tugged at the other's arm.

"In here. I hope you have strength enough to manage a short flight of most atrocious stairs."

"I can climb a greased ladder clear to the moon," the hunter said, "as long as I'm certain Indio's at the top."

"Bravo," the Colonel said. "And if that unspeakable lump of a tavern-keeper has carelessly barred the front door, I shall be sorely tempted to kick it off its leather hinges and drape it around his filthy neck."

He tried the door and swore disgustedly. "On the other hand, it would be an act of cruelty to awaken an honest barkeeper at so ungodly an hour, and we are involved in enough conflict without that. Fortunately, the second floor of this place is not too high."

He stepped back, reached up and caught the edge of the low balcony. Supressing a groan, he pulled himself up and swung his long legs over the railing. After a moment he reached down with both hands.

"Grab hold and grit your teeth. This won't be

pleasant but it will only be for a moment."

He dragged the other man up over the railing, then pushed open the window behind them. He scratched a match and lit a dim, foul-smelling oil lamp.

"Sit down and try to relax while I procure proper medicine." At the top of the stairway leading down to the tavern, the Colonel tried another grin. "In some ways, mine host is a remarkably careless man."

He came climbing back in a moment, carrying a bottle of whisky, nearly full, and two glasses. He poured generously. "Not the best, for sure, but adequate to loosen stiffened joints and muscles. Down, as they say, the hatch!"

Setting down his glass, the Colonel went to his valise and rummaged briefly in its depths. His hand emerged holding a full box of cartridges. He emptied half into his own hand and passed the remainder to his companion.

"I was never the one to put too much stock in luck, my boy, but the fact that you and I carry weapons of the identical calibre has seriously strained my scepticism. We'd have had one unholy beast of a time blowing these .44's up to fit a .45, or whittling them down to a .38 or, worse yet, reducing them to fit one of those ungodly European toys."

The two men finished reloading and tucked the remaining shells into their gunbelts. They tried a few fast draws, wincing at the agony of using bruised muscles but finding their speed not too greatly impaired.

"How about it now, lad?" the Colonel asked.

"You've limbered up quite a bit. Are you beginning to see the light?"

His companion attempted a twisted smile. "I'm starting to get a pretty fair idea of what that funny business was all about. I must have really been slugged silly not to have figured it out before. Now I'm cooking up some cute ways to meet and beat it."

"That isn't quite so urgent now," the Colonel said thoughtfully. "Even if worst comes to worst, the rest of the trail will be very short and we'll have more than enough money to see it to its end."

In the courtyard of the *hacienda,* Nino swallowed hard and looked at Indio. He licked his lips. "Indio, I know that you do not like to be asked questions but I am going crazy trying to figure out what it is we are doing."

The bandit chief grinned craftily, "Soon, my old and trusted friend. Soon all will be revealed to you. Now do the rest as you were directed."

Nino filled his lungs and uttered an ear-splitting, wordless yell of alarm. Indio winked at him, cupped hands to his mouth and bellowed, "Awake! Awake, you deaf dogs! Come out of there, damn your useless, slumbering souls."

There were muffled cries of alarm and then the band came tumbling from the storeroom, with Groggy and Cucillo in the lead. "What is it? What has happened, Indio? Has the posse found us? Must we shoot it out with the law?"

"It would be better to face a posse of lawmen,"

Indio said coldly, "than what exists here in our midst." He pointed. "You—Cucillo, Groggy, look in the shadow beneath that wall."

The two bandits moved forward cautiously, their faces puzzled as they searched the dark pocket Indio had sent them to. Cucillo was the one who suddenly yelped and jumped back as his feet encountered a yielding object. He bent over and peered nervously into the thinning area of darkness. "My God, it's Slim! He's dead and there's a knife stuck right through his heart. Who did it? Who killed him, Indio?"

The chieftain's voice was like the sound of ice floes grating together in the depth of winter. "The answer to your question should not be too hard to find. Each of us carries a knife of his own personal choosing, *amigos*. Each knife is different from the others for that very reason. So why do you not strike a match, *amigos*, and bend close—very, very close—so you can see if you could identify this knife?"

After a brief, puzzled hesitation, Cucillo raked a match along the wall and squatted down, peering into its light. Suddenly, he slapped his hand to his empty waist, uttered a high-pitched yelp and straightened like a jack-in-the-box.

"It's mine!" he quavered. "Mother of mercy, Indio, it's my knife. My initials are right there where I carved them, on the hilt."

"I had noticed that obvious point, *amigo*," Indio said, his voice without inflection. The bandit leader's hand went down and rested on the butt of his gun. "What a coincidence. What a curious coincidence,

Cucillo."

The outlaw goggled at Indio and then his whole body was suddenly wracked by a violent convulsion. His mouth opened and closed but no sound came forth. He flung out trembling hands toward the leader in a silent plea.

"I swear by all that's holy, Indio," he sobbed at last, "I have no idea how it came to be here. It was in my belt when I fell asleep. Only now did I discover it was missing, and Satan alone knows how it could possibly have gotten from my pants to—to where it is now."

Indio flicked his hand in gesture of supreme indifference. "Do not trouble your poor head about so small a problem, *chico*. It is all most simple, really. While you slept, dreaming, no doubt, of the great wealth that was about to be yours, your blade—that most devilish slice of steel, known for its unquenchable thirst for blood—was suddenly seized by a great desire to drink once more at the fountain. So, stealthily, it eased itself out of your belt, my good friend, and stole from the room. On feet as soundless as those of the hunting panther, it slipped outside and crept through the night in search of prey."

The bandit had collapsed on his knees, wringing his hands and gibbering incoherently. Indio sighed deeply and scratched his jaw with the butt of his pistol.

"All of a sudden," he went on with the story, "it peered through an open door and saw Slim—our ever-faithful Slim—maintaining his trusted vigilance. The sight was too much. Before Slim could cry out, it had pounced and was upon him, piercing the flesh, sucking out its fill of Slim's life blood."

Indio slid his gun back into its holster, put a boot on the low wall, just over the body of his dead comrade, and spread his hands, looking around at the hard faces of the others. "It is not difficult to understand, is it? We have all been in this business long enough to know how it can be, sometimes, with those naughty blades. The overpowering temptation is there—and then, wham! The awful deed is done and only much later can we feel the regret."

Cucillo wrung his hands, babbling hysterically. "No, no, no! You've got to believe me, Indio. I am innocent—innocent! Not once in the whole night did I leave that room, Indio. Only once was I awakened, Indio. It was all that wine I drank, demanding to be let out, but I went no further than the corner of the fireplace, Indio. I swear this to you. You must believe me, Indio. Don't play with me like this."

"I hear your words, Cucillo, old friend, but words are cheap. In such a circumstance, one must have proof. *Prove* to us that it was not your hand that drove your blade into Slim's heart."

"Prove it?" the bandit cried wildly. "How can I? What proof could there be? Nino? Tell him, Nino. Explain to Indio that it is impossible to prove such a thing."

Nino shrugged. Indio looked past the grovelling man at the hard faces of the watching bandits. "You see how it is when a man becomes greedy. His share of the money from the bank was not enough." His cold gaze went back to the terrified figure. "How much, Cucillo?

How much did the bounty killers promise you for cutting them loose and stealing back their guns?"

Groggy was the first to find his voice. "You mean those two are gone, Indio? He helped them get away?"

"Look for yourselves, *amigos*."

The bandits ran to the open door, then whirled back with yells of rage. Indio gestured sharply at the gibbering Cucillo. "For the sake of old times, my former friend, I will give you a chance for your life. Your horse is out there, around that corner. You are free to saddle up and ride away—if you can make it. Or would you rather I had someone count?"

The doomed man scrambled to his feet and ran, desperately, hopelessly. Indio let him get almost to the corner before he drew and fired.

The heavy slug caught Cucillo between the shoulder blades and hurled him into the dust. Indio kept firing until the gun was empty, the lifeless figure jerking to the tearing impact of the bullets.

When the hammer clicked on an empty shell, Indio dropped the gun back into its holster and stood looking down at the dead man. His shoulders heaved convulsively and a great, racking sob tore from his throat. He turned and flung himself against the wall, sobbing and whimpering, hammering the hard adobe with his fists.

After a time the spasm passed. Indio turned and saw the bandits still standing, rooted, staring at him. His face went dark with rage.

"What are you standing there for, you worthless dogs? Did you not hear what I said? Those bounty killers have escaped. I want them caught and brought back here—right now, right now, *right now!* They can't have gone far without their horses. Go get them and bring them back."

They moved then, running past Indio and Nino and out through the gate, to snatch up saddles and bridles and rifles. As the men vanished around the corner toward their tethered mounts, Indio cupped his hands to his mouth and bellowed, "Bring them back here, alive or dead, damn your worthless hides. And don't come back until you have them. I'll kill any man who dares show up empty-handed."

Indio stood listening until he heard the sound of running hoofbeats fading away. Then he turned and grinned at Nino.

"Well, now, old friend, has the picture become clearer for you? Do you begin to see my purpose in having you do those things you did tonight, things you did so well?"

Nino started to shake his head, his face still blank with bewilderment. Suddenly he stiffened, his eyes going wide with alarm.

"Indio! I just realised—there is one matter you have overlooked."

"I?" Indio said in mild surprise. "Indio has overlooked something in making his plans?"

"That one with the long coat and the splendid boots, Indio. The one they called the Colonel. He had his own room over in town, above the tavern."

"That is true, Nino, but I had not forgotten it."

"But—but, Indio, don't you see? His bag was in

that room and beyond a doubt there were spare bullets in that bag."

"Beyond a doubt, *amigo,*" Indio agreed placidly.

"Both wore guns of the same calibre. That means they will both be armed by now, and they are deadly shots. I think perhaps they are even better shots than any of your men."

"Unquestionably, old friend," Indio grinned, patting his shoulder. "But I am afraid *you* are the one who has overlooked the most important point of all."

Nino scratched his head helplessly. "I am more confused with every minute, Indio. Explain to me before my skull cracks wide open. What have *I* overlooked?"

"The fact, old friend, that it is very, very difficult for dead men to come back and demand their share of the loot."

CHAPTER 14

NINO stared at his chief, his jaw sagging. "Y-you mean . . . ?"

"Now understanding comes at last, eh, old friend?"

"If they are killed, then the money will all be ours—a whole million dollars. But the odds are thirteen against two in their favour, Indio. There is a chance that it will be the bounty killers who will die instead."

"Listen to me carefully, Nino," Indio said patiently. "It is all worked out so we cannot lose. If my men kill those two, they will return here with the bodies to prove their success. Is that not right?"

Nino nodded. "It is what I was trying to say."

"And if my men are killed, then those two will come back to kill us for the rewards. Is that not also correct?"

Nino threw out his hands in helpless confusion. Indio's grin widened.

"Either way, it will not matter in the slightest. For we will not be here. You and I, Nino, will be long gone and far, far away. Just two old and trusted friends—with a million dollars to share only with one another." He gave the other a shove. "Go and pack our things quickly while I get out the money from the chest. We have no time to waste."

Nino started across the grey-shadowed courtyard at

a trot. Suddenly, there was a faint, whistling sound. A glittering object flew through the air and struck Nino's back with an audible *thunk!* The big man took two more faltering steps, then pitched forward on to his face, a knife jutting between his shoulder blades.

From just beyond the low wall, the voice of the bandit known as Groggy spoke softly.

"Hold it right where you are, Indio." Groggy chuckled. "Not that you could do very much harm with an empty gun anyhow. You were a fool, my friend, to pump all those bullets into a man already dead and then forget to reload."

Groggy came through the gate, grinning, his gun cocked and levelled in a rock-steady hand. He reached over cautiously and got the empty weapon from Indio's holster. "Just in case, my old and trusted friend. You always were the great one for tricks."

"Why aren't you with the others?" Indio snarled.

"Because, my friend, I'm not as stupid as the others. To me, your game was just a little too obvious. I decided to sit tight until it came my turn to deal. Now I've got all the cards."

"Then get it over with, damn you," Indio growled hoarsely.

"Oh, no, Mr. Tricky Indio. Business before pleasure. For all I know, you could have all kinds of traps planted around to guard that chest. You're going to open it and you're going to take out all those beautiful bank notes. Only when they're in my hands, will it be time to deal you out."

Indio half-lifted his hands, then let them drop. "All

right Groggy. I'll admit that for once you've outsmarted me."

"You bet I have, *amigo*. That was a pretty elaborate plan you cooked up, so that there'd be only two persons to share that million dollars. Elaborate and clever. But I've worked out a scheme that's even more clever, *old friend*. In my scheme the money doesn't have to be shared at all. It's all going to belong to one man—and I'm going to let you guess who that one man is going to be."

"Look, Groggy," Indio said earnestly. "You've got the upper hand, but there are some things you haven't taken into consideration, things I've got all carefully thought out."

"As carefully as you had this trick thought out, Indio? You overlooked one little thing here, remember? Me."

"Listen to me, Groggy, and *think*. If we ride out of here together, I can take you straight to the one spot in the country where we can live to spend every penny of that million dollars. If you try to go it alone, without the plans I've got all worked out, you'll be lucky to last a week."

"You know," the other said thoughtfully, "I never thought the day would come when I'd see the almighty Indio trying to dicker for his miserable life. I used to dream about it but I never really believed I'd see it." He shook his head in wonder.

"One week, Groggy, and you'll be all finished."

"You don't know me well, Indio. I can have one helluva big time and spend one helluva lot of money in just one week. After that, who knows? I could get bit by a rattlesnake or choke to death on a *tortilla.*"

Groggy gestured sharply with his gun. "Get going, Indio, and don't bother asking a stupid question like 'where?' And show some speed. My head may not be worth anywhere near as much as yours but I don't intend to hang around until it winds up tied to a bounty killer's saddle."

Keeping a safe distance, Groggy followed his captive to the strong room door and watched him get out a huge key. The door groaned open. Indio took a stump of candle from a niche beside the door and lit it. Holding it high, he went into the small, pitch-black room.

The chest was on the far side, hemmed in by boxes and barrels of grain and other stores. Indio stood for a long moment, staring at it. Then he went down on one knee and took the key from around his neck.

Groggy remained in the doorway, still fearful of a trap of some kind or even a suicidal, bare-handed attack by the desperate bandit. His cold, narrowed eyes followed every move Indio made and his gun pointed steadily at the other's back.

"Hurry up," Groggy snarled. "Open it!"

The key grated and the huge padlock fell open. Indio let it drop to the dirt floor and slowly lifted the lid.

For the space of a dozen heartbeats not a muscle of his crouching body moved. He seemed completely frozen, staring down into the big box.

Suddenly a great, tearing rasp of wild laughter burst

from Indio's lips. His body began to rock back and forth, head thrown back, mouth straining wide, while peal after peal of mad, mocking laughter howled from his throat.

Colonel Douglas Mortimer was down on one knee, rummaging in his valise again. He stood up and came back to the table, carrying the big Bible. Its heavy covers were heavily embossed, the title stamped in gold leaf. The hunter said nothing but his eyebrows climbed a notch.

"A man," the Colonel said, "must have at least one thing in his life in which he can put his absolute trust, my boy. I have trusted my life to this volume many, many times and never once has it let me down. Having it near always gives me a feeling of complete security."

He opened the cover and turned the printed pages, pausing to read a passage here, a verse there. The other sat up sharply, staring. After the first few printed chapters, the pages were completely blank. The Colonel's hand turned another page and the younger man's mouth flew open.

"I'll—be—damned!"

The remainder of the thick volume had been hollowed out and the rectangular cavity lined with soft velvet. Nestling against the velvet, held in place by spring clips, were two little, pearl-handled, single-shot derringers. The Colonel handed one to his companion and tucked the other into his vest pocket.

"These might come in handy before this day is ended. I have discovered that when a desperate adversary is keeping count and hears you fire six shots in close succession, he frequently exhibits a tendency to become a wee bit careless about exposing his person."

The other grinned faintly and got to his feet. "It seems our minds kind of run in the same channels, Colonel."

The Man With No Name pulled the tail of the brown poncho around and tipped the corner back. Sewn to the inside of the stout fabric, just above the line of fringe, was a miniature holster containing a somewhat plainer, but equally deadly, derringer.

"I thought some of using it out there last night, but I finally gave the idea up. The one shot would only kill one of them, anyhow, and I couldn't see much point in giving the rest of the gang the excuse they needed for finishing us off then and there."

The Colonel prodded a swollen cheekbone and winced. "You were right, but for a time there, I got to almost wishing they would finish us off and get it over with. But after a while I just got too numb to feel much of anything they did to me."

He leaned over and blew out the flickering lamp. Grey daylight filtered in from the brightening eastern sky. The Colonel went to the open window and peered cautiously up the street.

"They're coming at last. Indio must have made quite a production out of his little act to have held up the pursuit this long."

"Better late than never," the younger man said. "I've got all the patience in the world when its the big pay-wagon of my life I'm waiting for."

"That little spread upcountry means about everything to you, doesn't it, my boy?"

"Enough." The hunter ventured a quick look out the window. "They're bunched up at the end of the street now, looking this way and talking things over. It's my guess they take a slow ride completely around the town first, looking for our tracks leading out. They'd be almighty unhappy if they wasted half a day hunting for us around here and then discovered we'd simply gone right on through and kept travelling."

The Colonel put on his black hat and long frock coat. He gave his pistol an experimental twitch to verify its free movement in the waxed holster.

"What do you say, my boy? Shall we go down and meet that big pay-wagon? Or shall we sit down and have another drink and wait for it to come to us?"

CHAPTER 15

GROGGY went across the floor in two bounds, his former wariness forgotten. He stood over the chest, eyes bulging, gaping down at the reward poster, at the face that laughed back at him from the depths of its emptiness. At his feet the flesh-and-blood face of Indio unconsciously mimicked the painted face as it flung out gusts of crazy laughter.

Groggy cursed in a high, shrill whinny and his boot lashed out. His former chief fell over the corner of the chest and sprawled on the dirt floor, the laughter choking off.

"Where is it?" Groggy screamed, his eyes wild. "Speak up, goddam you! Where did you hide it?"

"I haven't touched it," Indio gasped, his voice still bubbling with unholy mirth. "Oh, what a gorgeous, glorious joke. Don't you get the joke yet, my good friend, Groggy? *They* took the money—those two. The bounty killers got it, Groggy. They took it and left the reward poster in its place so I'd be sure to appreciate the joke. Oh, never, never was there a joke so rich, so priceless." He rocked again, burbling helplessly.

"You're lying, damn you!" Groggy yelled wildly. "You're lying through your double-crossing teeth. There was only *one* key to the strongroom, wasn't there, Indio? And only *one* key to the chest, wasn't there? The locks weren't broken, were they? So how could *they* get it out, eh?"

Groggy bent and clawed his free hand into Indio's jacket, dragging the bandit leader to his knees, shaking him furiously. "Answer me, damn you! *How—did—they—get—it—out*?"

Then Groggy straightened up, panting, his body shaking uncontrollably. "Of course. All that money just got lonesome lying in there all by itself, didn't it? So it just slipped out and went for a long stroll—like Cucillo's knife. That's how it really happened, didn't it, Indio? Tell me about it, just the way you told Cucillo about his knife, Indio. Come, come! I'm dying to hear you tell it in your own way, old friend."

Indio beat his hands against this thighs, rocked back and forth and gave vent to another wild paroxysm of crazy laughter. Between gales, he gasped, "Why didn't you ask *them*—the bounty killers—how the million dollars got out and what they did with it, Groggy? Hurry and you may find them before the others do. Just ask them nicely, Groggy, the way you asked me, and I'm sure they'll be only too happy to tell you where it is now."

Groggy cursed wildly and whirled away. He ran around the small room, kicking open crates and boxes, overturning barrels in his search. He slashed his knife across leather sacks, hanging from the rafters. Rice, corn and barley gushed out to mingle with dried onions, garlic, turnips, pumpkins and slabs of dried beef littering the floor.

Indio hunkered on the floor and watched Groggy. The outlaw leader was still rocking and choking with laughter. Only now when he laughed, great tears squeezed out to trickle down his face.

They both froze simultaneously, listening to the first burst of gunfire from somewhere along the street of Agna Caliente.

"It won't be long now, Groggy, my dear old friend," Indio giggled. "They will finish up and be here soon, looking for you and me. There is still time to run, Groggy."

"I'm not leaving, damn you," Groggy screamed. "I'm not getting out until I find that million dollars."

Indio laid a finger alongside his nose and winked craftily. "I'll give you a little hint, Groggy. It's buried in a grave somewhere, *amigo*—the same way you will be before the sun sets tonight."

Groggy glared at Indio through bloodshot eyes. "There are other places to hide it around here, plenty of them. And I'm not leaving until I've searched every one, you rat. I'm locking you in here for now because I can't search and keep an eye on you at the same time. But I'll be watching, so don't dig up any hidden gun or try any tricks. And don't try to break out and sneak away. I'll follow and kill you."

"I won't be leaving here," Indio said.

"I *know* you won't, old friend," Groggy said. He bared his teeth in a death's head grin. "After the others rode off this morning, I took the precaution of cutting your horse loose from the tether and driving it away."

He turned at the doorway. "My horse is the only one left, Indio, and he's well hidden—perhaps as well hidden as the million dollars. Besides, he's very spooky. He's been trained to turn killer if anyone tries to ride him but me."

An ordinary man would have heard no sound at all, but the hunter's hearing had been tuned extra-fine by the demands of his hazardous trade. Now he flattened against the adobe wall, his gun ready, the hammer drawn back and restrained only by the ball of his thumb. The furtive steps whispered closer and closer.

The Man With No Name flung himself away from the wall and fell to his knees to foil an adversary who would be aiming chest high.

"Oh, hell," he said disgustedly and got to his feet, easing his gun hammer down gently. "If we keep going like this, we'll wind up shooting each other's fool heads off."

"I agree," Colonel Mortimer said, lowering his own pistol. "From now on we'd better stay together—or at least keep each other in sight at all times."

"Suppose I take the other side of the street and keep pace with you. That way I can keep an eye on the roofs over your head and you can do the same above mine."

"Fair enough," the Colonel said. "The first thing they'd do is split up, so there must be six or seven of them somewhere behind the buildings on either side. Undoubtedly, some of these hovels have rear entrances, so any door or window could be hiding an amb . . ."

The hunter's hard shoulder drove into the Colonel's chest, driving the air from his lungs and knocking him backward. The older man's boot heels caught on a plank of the sidewalk and he landed on his back with the hunter slamming down across his knees.

Simultaneously, a gun racketed and a slug pounded into the adobe wall at the spot where the Colonel had been standing. The hunter twisted around and fired. Across the street, a bandit let his pistol drop, sagged forward and pitched off the edge of a low roof. He landed heavily in the street and lay motionless, the pale dust smoking up around his body.

The two bounty killers scrambled up, looking warily around for other enemies. The hunter tipped out the cylinder of his gun and replaced the spent shell.

"Thank you, my boy," the Colonel said. "I'll welcome the opportunity to do as much for you."

"I'll expect it," the other said. He squinted at the figure in the street. "The one they called Tio, I think. Small fry. Not over a thousand, as I recall. What do you make our score so far, counting the hunchback? Financially, I mean."

"I haven't any idea, boy," the Colonel said. "I hadn't though of keeping tally on the bounties."

The tall man shook his head sadly. "Sometimes, Colonel, you just don't strike me as being a practical man."

They separated and moved slowly along the street,

each keeping close to the buildings on his side. Their heads moved constantly from side to side, their eyes shuttling to probe every nook and cranny. At each closed door and shuttered window they flattened to the wall and waited for long minutes, listening intently before darting past.

Behind the hunter, a door inched softly open and the muzzle of a gun poked through the crack, centring carefully on the broad, ponchoed back. Across the street, the Colonel's big pistol slammed. White splinters leaped from the door. The gun vanished from the crack and clattered to the floor inside.

The tall man whirled. Standing close to the wall, he reached out and gave the door a hard shove with the barrel of his gun. It swung part way, then bumped against some obstruction. The Man With No Name peered cautionsly through the opening and turned away, holding up one finger.

"Even Steven," he said.

They reached the end of the short street and turned to face each other. "What's the next move, Colonel?"

"If the mountain won't come to Mohammed, then Mohammed doesn't have much choice. I'm going to have a look around behind these shanties."

"I better stay out where I can cover both sides of the street, then. And Colonel, try not to shoot over in this direction if you can help it. That damn cannon of yours has too long a range for me to feel altogether comfortable when you're out of sight."

The Colonel tipped his gun in acknowledgment and ducked from view around the corner of the last building. After a few moments there was a flurry of gunfire—several shots close together, a pause, a single shot, then silence.

The hunter stood listening, frowning, considering whether or not to leave his post to investigate. Two guns up the street made the decision for him.

They racketed almost in unison and he felt the hot breath of the slugs slam past his face as he whirled. He was a shade too late to get off a shot at the pair who ducked back into a narrow passageway between buildings. Keeping his eyes on the aperture, the hunter backed slowly into a shallow doorway.

Down the street, part of a *sombrero* poked into view. The tall man snorted, holding his fire.

"The oldest trick in the book," he muttered disgustedly, "but those jug-heads probably think they invented it."

He waited, squeezing back further so that only his gun and one eye would clear the edge. At the added pressure, the door at his back creaked open. He whirled, his gun swinging to cover every point in the small room. The room was in heavy shadows, with shutters covering its lone window, but the hunter saw at once that it was empty and devoid of any hiding place.

He also saw that it was a primitive barber shop. Its sparse furnishings consisted of a bench along one wall, a high-backed wooden chair in the centre, and a coat rack in the corner opposite the door. A rude shelf held a shaving mug and brush, a razor, a pair of shears and a dirty comb.

A glitter came into the hunter's narrowed eyes. He turned and slammed the door shut with a crash that shook the room.

The noise echoed along the street. Two bandits darted out from their cover and ran toward the little shop, their eyes hot with anticipation. They flattened themselves at each side of the door, their guns cocked and levelled. One nodded and the other swung his foot and kicked the door wide open.

Even in the shadowed room, there was no mistaking the tall figure, the brown poncho topped by the flat-crowned black hat. The bandits fired together from the doorway at point-blank range, the brown poncho jerking at the impact of their bullets.

The hunter leaned around the concealing back of the barber chair and fired two close-spaced shots. Then he went to the coat rack where he had carefully draped his poncho and ruefully inspected the bullet holes. He put it on, donned his hat and stepped to the doorway.

He turned the bodies over with the toe of his boot and studied the faces, frozen in expressions of utter astonishment. His lips moved in silent calculation and a look of pleasant surprise came over his face. He stepped over the two men and went out into the street.

The key grated in the lock and the door of the strongroom swung open. Groggy came in, holding his gun. His face was contorted and his eyes were wild.

Indio was still seated on the floor in the same spot Groggy has last seen him, but now his face was calm, his eyes bright. He was leaning on his right arm, his left being out of sight behind the corner of the chest.

"So you found nothing, old friend, as I told you," was Indio's greeting. "Now perhaps you will believe that somehow—who can say how?—those two bounty killers got away with the money."

Groggy seemed not to have heard him. He cried, hoarsely, "My horse! It's gone! It pulled up its picket pin and wandered off somewhere." He glared at the other man, his mouth working. "Do you understand? I'm trapped here—the same as you are now."

Indio bent his head, listening to the distant hammer of gunfire. "Then, *amigo,* we had better stop fighting with each other and begin to plan how we can fight together against those two when they arrive."

"Yes," Groggy said. "Yes, Indio. There's nothing for us to quarrel about now. Here . . ." He snatched Indio's pistol from the waistband of his trousers, checked the loads and tossed it to the seated man. Indio reached up languidly and caught the gun with his right hand. Then he brought his left hand into view, holding a second pistol. Groggy stared at it open-mouthed, his eyes bulging.

"I have told you over and over again that you are a fool, Groggy. Now maybe you will begin to believe me. Nobody but a fool would snatch the weapon from an enemy's holster and think him disarmed without looking beneath his jacket for a second gun tucked in his belt. That is why you would not last a week if left to depend on your own wits."

Indio scrambled up, tucking one gun under his jacket, dropping the other into its holster. Groggy's eyes lost some of their fear. "What'll we do?"

"I have been studying the problem since you left and I believe I see a way to catch those two in a cross-fire not even they can survive."

CHAPTER 16

Colonel Douglas Mortimer edged closer to the rear corner of the last building on the street, then paused to reconnoitre. A low wall of adobe, about three feet high, extended back some distance from the building at his side, then made a right-angle turn. A quick glance around the corner showed him that the wall formed two sides of a large stable yard. The stable itself stood at the far end of the yard.

It was a large two-storey structure, its double doors standing open. Above these a smaller door also stood open on a half-filled hayloft. The yard slanted sharply down from the wall to the stable. A loaded freight wagon, parked by the wall in front of the Colonel, had its rear axle lashed to a tree to prevent it from rolling down against the stable doors.

The Colonel risked another quick look around the corner and ducked back a split second before the gunfire stung his face. He dropped to his hands and scuttled along below the shielding wall until he estimated himself to be almost opposite the parked wagon.

He peered cautiously over the wall. A bandit knelt by a heavy wooden watering trough, jamming bullets into his pistol. The outlaw snapped the cylinder back into place, cocked the hammer and lifted his head to look toward the corner of the building. Colonel Mortimer shot him neatly between the eyes.

The Colonel ducked back when he heard the sudden pound of running feet, then looked again. Two more bandits had just vanished into the stable, pulling the heavy door shut behind them. He heard the thud of a bar dropping into place to lock the door.

Presently, the Colonel caught a flicker of movement in the shadows of the hayloft. He threw himself down an instant before two shots glanced off the top of the wall, showering him with dust. Scrambling around, he went back to the corner where he could stand erect.

Reloading, he cocked the long gun and levelled it at the taut rope restraining the wagon. He took a long time settling the sights on their tiny target, using his left hand to lend extra steadiness to his right.

The gun thundered and bucked in his hand and the taut rope parted with a sharp *twang*. The wagon wheels creaked and began to turn, slowly at first and then steadily faster. The heavy vehicle rumbled down the slope, picking up speed and momentum with every yard, and struck the closed doors of the stable dead centre.

The heavy planking vanished in a cloud of flying splinters. The wagon careened on across the stable, snapping off a row of posts supporting the hayloft above, and crashing into the rear wall. From overhead came the groan of straining timber; there was a rending crackle and then the whole floor collapsed. Tons of hay came cascading down and with it the yelling figures of two bandits.

They landed hard and rolled out through the shattered doors, arms and legs flailing the dust. Colonel Mortimer propped one booted foot on the low wall, rested his gun hand on his knee and relieved the pair of their earthly tribulations with two well-placed shots.

He reloaded and was snapping the cylinder back into place when his eye caught a flicker of movement. A man was coming from around the stable, running behind the wall. He was ducking low, but not quite low enough. A heavy slug from the Colonel's long-barrelled pistol took off the entire back of his head.

Mortimer vaulted the wall and walked the length of the yard, seeing no further sign of an enemy. But from beyond the row of buildings fronting the street came a muffled rattle of gunfire. The Colonel rounded the last building and stepped back into the street, looking around.

The tall figure of his partner was backing out of an open door, dragging the body of a bandit by the collar. He dropped the outlaw beside a row of similar bodies, straightened and saw the frockcoated figure approaching.

"Howdy. It kind of looks as if I've gunned myself plumb out of business on this side, Colonel. How about you?"

"It appears that I've done the same. Let's add up the tally and see if any are unaccounted for."

The hunter ticked off the count on his fingers and shook his head, frowning. "We seem to be two short, not counting Indio. I didn't see hide nor hair of either Nino or that one they call Groggy."

"Not among my kills either. They might be hiding out somewhere here in town, but it's more likely they're out at the *hacienda* with Indio."

"There's one good way to find out. Let's go."

Groggy crouched by the window, gun in hand, peering out through the crack between the shutters. His face was ghost-pale and sweat glittered on his forehead. Behind him, Indio sat on a box, turning the thick gold watch in his hands. He snapped up the lid and the tinkle of chimes filled the room. Groggy turned his head.

"You and that damn watch. I never saw anybody so *loco* over that *tinkle-tinkle* as you."

There was no response. Indio's head was tipped forward, his eyes closed, his face gone slack. Behind the closed lids he was once more seeing those moments out of the past in vivid detail.

He could hear the sharp ripping sound as he tore away the thin gown to expose the nude, quivering body of the young girl on the bed. He shook again with the fierce, hot lust to possess her. Then he was upon her, everything but his animal need forgotten. He was not even aware that his gun had dropped from his hand and lay beside the pillow.

The racketing thunder of the gunshot so close to his ear broke the spell that had consumed him. He yelled and flung himself off the bed, looking wildly down at his body for the first sign of blood. It took him a full minute to absorb the fact that he had not been hit.

Only then did he look at the girl on the bed and see the blackened bullet hole under her left breast. As he stared, the blood appeared, bubbling up. He cursed crazily, whirled around and lurched out into the night.

On the bed, the dead girl's hand still clutched the pistol with which she had taken her broken life. Engraved deep on its butt plate was the name of its owner—Indio.

Rough hands were suddenly shaking and slapping him. The voice of Groggy rasped against his ears.

"Wake up! Come out of it, damn you! Can't you understand what I'm telling you, you crazy fool? They're coming, both of them. They're coming to get us, now."

CHAPTER 17

THE hunter pointed into the courtyard at the sprawling figure; there was a knife jutting from its back.

"Scratch Nino," he said. "We didn't even have to spend the price of a bullet to collect that five thousand."

Colonel Mortimer looked at his partner as if he had not heard the words. His face had gone cold and tight, his eyes were like pale chips of agate.

"Listen to me carefully," the Colonel said. "The bounty means nothing to me, but Indio himself is mine and mine alone. I've come too far and waited too many years for this moment to be robbed of it now. Don't try to interfere or shoot him yourself. I'll kill anyone who tries to get in my way now. Even . . . a friend!"

The hunter looked at the Colonel for a long moment, without expression on his dark face.

"He's all yours."

The Man With No Name stopped, letting the other stride through the gate in the low wall. In the middle of the courtyard the Colonel halted, the long pistol held down at his side.

"Indio," he shouted. "I know you're in there somewhere. Listen to me. This is Colonel Mortimer—Colonel Douglas Mortimer of Carolina. Does that name mean anything to you?"

He stood for long moments, waiting, listening.

"All right, Indio. If the name doesn't, here's something that will. Remember, a long time ago, a bridal bedroom. A young boy on the floor, chest smashed by bullets. A young girl on the bed, ravished and dead by her own hand on her wedding night."

He waited patiently, listening to the silence.

"You took the watch that was her wedding present. Indio! You took the watch, but you left behind the gun with your name on it. It's been a long and bitter trail, Indio, but here is where it comes to its end."

In the shadowy room, Indio stood up slowly, moving like a man in a trance, his face slack, his eyes muddy. Holding the gold watch in his left hand, he drew his pistol with the right and looked down at both objects, as if they were things he had never seen before.

Staring at him wildly, Groggy bleated, "Indio! I don't know what's come over you but for God's sake, come out of it. Indio—your plan. Remember? Your plan to get them in a crossfire. Indio, can't you get it through your head that our time is running out?"

Indio gave no sign that he heard. He looked down at his pistol again, spinning the cylinder with his thumb to check the loads. He looked up at his shaking companion.

"Groggy, unbar the door."

"No, Indio," the other yelped. "You've gone crazy. You're going out to face him. You'll get yourself killed and then they'll come in here and kill me. You're crazy, Indio—stark, staring mad. My God, I'm trapped between a madman and two killers."

Groggy swung his head from side to side, his face working. Then his strained nerves gave way completely. With a strangled yell of sheer terror, he ran to a rear window, tore open the shutters and dived out.

He struck the ground, rolled over and scampered off. Running desperately in blind panic, he dashed across the open space between the strongroom building and the stables. The hunter's gun slammed. The bandit pitched forward, slid on his face and lay still.

The sound of the shot brought Indio out of his daze. He darted to the front window and knelt to peer out between the shutters. Through the narrow space he could see the tall figure in the frock coat waiting, his gun held out a little from his side.

Indio laid the barrel of his pistol on the window ledge. He took a long time aiming before he let the hammer fall. The thunder of the shot was echoed by the *spang* of metal against metal. A numbing shock enveloped the Colonel's arm. The long-barrelled pistol went spinning out of his hand to land a dozen feet away.

The shutters crashed open and Indio stood framed in the opening, his gun levelled. "Don't move!"

He climbed out carefully, never taking his burning gaze off the other man. He stopped a few paces away and held up the gold watch.

"We'll do it your way, Colonel, since you're so dead set on it. Man to man." Indio slid his own pistol back into its holster. "When the chimes run down and stop, see if you can make it to your gun in time."

The Colonel's cold gaze shifted to his fallen pistol, gauging the distance. Indio laughed.

"Think you can make it, Colonel, in time to shoot me?"

The lid of the watch snapped open and the thin tinkle of the chimes rang out. The hunter stepped from behind a corner of the stable, his gun levelled, his left hand closed around a hidden object.

"I don't think he's even going to try, Indio."

The bandit's hand started for his own gun and froze at the cold menace in the tall man's eyes. The Man With No Name walked to the Colonel. "His slug might have damaged something in the mechanism of your gun. You'd better use mine instead."

He reached under the poncho, freed the buckle and brought out his belt with a holstered gun. The Colonel dropped his own empty belt and put the other around his waist. He flexed his hand a few times to make sure the numbness had passed.

"It won't be as fast as your cross-belly draw, Colonel. You sure you can take it anyhow?"

The Colonel nodded. "I make it a point to keep in practice either way."

"One other little thing," the tall man said. "I'll do the timing this time, Indio, and I prefer to do it with *this.*"

He opened his left hand to disclose a duplicate of the watch Indio was holding. Colonel Mortimer's jaw dropped. His hand dipped into his vest pocket and he stared blankly at the empty watch chain. He looked at the younger man. "You?"

"Yeah. Up in your room this morning you got a little too careless, Colonel, and I got a little too curious. I had to try to figure out what the business with the watch was all about."

Indio was staring from one watch to the other, an expression of blank wonder on his swarthy features.

"Yes, Indio," the Colonel said. "They're duplicates, both from the same firm of watchmakers in Switzerland. I bought mine first. She was so utterly enchanted with it that I sent off for another and gave it to her as a wedding present." Knots of muscle moved along his jaw line. "She didn't have very long to enjoy it, did she, Indio?"

The bandit snapped the lid of his watch shut, cutting off the sweet, tinkling melody. He let his left hand drop to his side. Beads of sweat crawled from his hairline and down over his forehead. His tongue came out to wet his lips.

The hunter stepped back to one side. "Time to start the music," he said quietly and opened the watch he had taken from the Colonel. He lifted his gun warningly. "Don't get over eager, Indio. Make sure you wait for the very last chime."

Now that he no longer had the big advantage over his opponent, Indio's nerves began to feel the strain. As the melody tinkled on the tension mounted. Indio shifted his feet in the dust, licked his lips. His breathing grew shorter and more audible. His eyes shifted constantly from one to the other of the cold-eyed pair, looking vainly for a ray of hope.

The Colonel stood as motionless as a statue, his face devoid of all expression. The hunter watched Indio with a steady, burning gaze.

The chimes were running down at last, the notes falling more and more slowly on the aching silence. Indio lifted his right hand and scrubbed the palm against the front of his shirt, wiping off what he could of the perspiration.

A thin note came, a dragging pause, and then the final *tink*. Indio's hand flashed down with the speed of a striking snake, his gun seeming almost to leap up to meet his grasp.

Colonel Mortimer drew and shot from the hip. Indio spun around and fell heavily. His gun bounced out of a hand gone suddenly limp. His body threshed convulsively for a moment, almost as if he were trying to rise. His hand twitched toward his fallen weapon. Then the last fierce struggle to retain a hold on life came to an end and his body went limp and still.

The Colonel dropped the borrowed gun into its holster and picked up his own pistol. He examined, tested the mechanism and slipped it into the holster above his left hip.

"No harm done. The slug glanced off the front of the trigger guard. It's a wonder it didn't tear my finger off."

He leaned down, put his boot on the dead bandit's left hand and wrenched the gold watch free. He looked at it for a long time, then put it in his pocket. The hunter shut the lid of the one he was holding and extended his hand.

"I'll trade this for my gun and belt, Colonel. A man can't very well hang up his gun and get out of this business if he doesn't have a gun."

Colonel Mortimer unbuckled the heavy belt and handed it over. "Many thanks for the loan, my boy. It came at a most opportune time."

The other flicked a salute from the broad brim of his hat. "Don't mention it, old man. You put it to the best possible use. We'll consider that the interest on the loan."

The Colonel attached his own watch to its chain and put it away. "Well, I suppose we might as well start cleaning up the mess."

They found their horses in the stable. In a box stall at the opposite end stood a pair of work horses. "Well, well," the hunter said, looking pleased. "And I noticed a wagon out behind that's just the right size to hold the evidence we'll have to show in order to collect the rewards."

As they finished harnessing and hitching the team, the Colonel said, "I think it would be a nice thing to first collect the ones in Agua Caliente proper. That will show the local citizens that the war has ended and it is now safe to come out from behind their walls and take up their interrupted business."

"That's fine with me," the younger man agreed, "but I'm taking Indio right along with us. That's one carcass I'm not letting out of my sight until the ten thousand is right in my little hand."

They dumped Indio's heavy body in the wagon like a side of beef and climbed into their saddles. They rode back to the town, leading the team between them. By the time they had collected all the scattered corpses, the wagon was half full.

Back at the *hacienda* they added the bodies of Nino and Slim to their wagonload. Colonel Douglas Mortimer stepped back, eyed the load briefly, then gathered up the reins of his black horse. He extended his hand.

"Congratulations, my boy. You've made that dream of yours come true at last. You've become an extremely wealthy man."

The other stared at him blankly. "You mean *we've* become wealthy men."

The Colonel smiled faintly and shook his head. "It's all yours, lad. You earned it and you richly deserve it. I got the one thing I was really after when Indio died with my bullet in his heart."

"Now, just wait a minute, Colonel . . ."

"My boy, you know exactly what you would do with a large sum of money. Frankly, I wouldn't have the faintest idea what I would do with any more than I already have or can earn along the way."

"But what about our partnership, our agreement?"

The Colonel snapped his fingers, looking annoyed. "Dear me, it must be my age. I seem to be getting absent-minded in my declining years. I completely forgot to tell you that I dissolved our partnership a little while ago, over there in the courtyard. Perhaps I'll drop around to see that little spread upcountry some day and we'll talk about forming some sort of a new one."

The other swallowed with an effort. "About taking your watch, Colonel. I'm—I'm sorry."

The older man brushed the apology aside with a gesture. "No harm done at all. Your action was quite understandable under the rather unusual circumstances. If our positions had been reversed it is not at all impossible that I might have done the same as you." He swung up into his saddle.

"Colonel, that photograph inside the lid. Such a lovely face. It—it seemed to me I could detect just a trace of family resemblance in it."

"That would not be entirely unusual, my boy. In fact, it is fairly frequent with brothers and sisters." The Colonel touched his hat in parting salute. *"Adios,* my boy. *Hasta la vista."*

The hunter watched the tall, erect back for a moment, then turned to the wagon. He began counting the bodies, totalling up the rewards as he identified each. He reached twenty thousand and stopped, scratching his head, his face twisted into a puzzled frown.

Behind him something rustled, ever so faintly. He dropped into a crouch and whirled, drawing and firing in an unbelievably fast movement. The body of the bandit Groggy sagged forward and pitched on its face.

The Man With No Name holstered his gun, a grin of relief breaking the grimness of his face. "Twenty-*seven* thousand," he murmured.

The tall figure on the black horse had twisted in his saddle at the sound of the gunshot. He cupped hands to his mouth. "Any trouble back there, son?"

"Not any more, Colonel," the other shouted back. "I thought for a minute my arithmetic had gone plumb sour on me. But it's all cleared up now. I got my total to come out exactly right."

The hunter went to Groggy's body and turned it over. There were two bloodstains on the bandit's shirt front, the older one higher up and nearer the shoulder. The hunter straightened disgustedly.

"Hell, I only *winged* the buzzard with my first shot. It's plain I've got to take a few days off and sharpen up my shooting eye with a little practice."

He dragged the body to the wagon and flopped it onto the pile. He tied his bay to the tail-gate, climbed up on the wagon seat and slapped the lines. The team lurched into the harnesses and the wagon moved.

Around the end of the building that housed the bandit's strongroom, the Man With No Name stopped the wagon under a low, spreading tree. Looking back, he saw the Colonel's figure grow tiny in the distance.

He reached up and took the bulging saddlebags from the branch on which they had landed the night before. He held them in his lap and patted them gently, affectionately.

"Forty thousand more to go into the kitty," he said softly. "It isn't like keeping the whole million—but then even a few dollars more can make a mighty lot of difference."